Forever Ours

The Forever Series

Emma L Stevens

Enjoy!

Love

Emma xx

Please feel free to contact Author: emmalstevensauthor@gmail.com

No artificial intelligence (AI) was used in the writing or publication of this work.

Editor: Pinpoint editing

Proofread by: Eros Edits.

Cover Design by: Ever After PR

Character Art: Krida Studios

Illustrations: Faye Sterling

Content Warning

Organised crime. Stalking - off-page. Alcohol Consumption. Blackmail. Kidnapping and captivity - off-page. Controlling behaviour. Death of a parent - off-page. Murder - off-page. Swearing. Explicit sexual consent. Sexism and Misogyny. Gun violence. Emotional abuse. Violence, fighting (not MMC). Kidnapping - off-page. (Not FMC).

This book is **18+**

Some contents of this book may be triggering for different people, and please feel free to message me if you think I have missed any.

emmalstevensauthor@gmail.com

Author's Note

Please note: This series is set in London and it written in British English.

Life is about proving people wrong.

Chapter 1

Isabella

"There's no way we're standing in this queue," I say, gazing up at the glass panels stretching from floor to ceiling, soft vibrations from the music within beating against our feet. "Let's just go somewhere else."

"Hell no!" Sam twists to face me, her eyes pleading. "When do we ever get the opportunity to come to a place like this?"

The streets are buzzing with people ready to enjoy their night. Soho has always been known for its vibrant nightlife, and tonight I can finally say we are going to experience it after weeks—months—of planning this night.

Our close friend, Beth, works at Death by Kiss, one of the most exclusive nightclubs in the area, and she's finally managed to get our names on the increasingly exclusive list.

Chloe sighs next to me, tugging the hem of her navy-blue dress down. "By the time we get in there, it's going to be pointless."

Six security guards monitor the queue, which disappears past the huge, glass panels and around the corner.

"Fine." I scoff. "But if you moan once about those heels hurting you, I can promise there will be a slap coming your way."

"I promise. Hey, I'll even do the washing up for a week. How about that?"

I shoot her a look, because we all know that won't be the case.

"Come on, Chlo," I say, squeezing her hand. "If we hate it, we can grab a pizza on the way home and binge-watch *Benidorm*?"

"Double pepperoni, stuffed crust?" Chloe gives me a pointed look.

"A family size, just for yourself," I say, wiggling my eyebrows, and I know I've got her.

Sam hums as she taps her nail against her front tooth. "Right, fuck this!" she announces a little too loudly, gaining the attention of the girls in front of us.

Grabbing our hands, she tugs us out of the queue and strides towards the front.

"Well, what do we have here then?" a security guard with a gold tooth asks as we reach him. Amusement dances behind his eyes as they flick between us. His arms are the size of my head, and when he notices me looking, he flexes them.

Oh, dude, it takes a little more than muscles to impress me.

It's a good start, though.

"We're here to get in," Sam says, oblivious to his charms.

"You and everybody else, sweetheart." He crosses his arms over his chest, unfazed.

"Our names are on the list."

"You. And. Every. Body. Else," he repeats, bending so he's eye-level with Sam.

"I don't care about everybody else ..." She pauses, waiting for him to tell her his name.

"Jake," he offers, arching a brow.

"Jake."

Jake's eyes sparkle. He may have met his match.

"Look, sweetheart. If I let you jump the queue ..." His words die in his mouth as his eyes flick behind us, and he stands up straight. "Mr. Barone. Mr. Ross. Nice to see you."

"Jake," a deep voice says behind us, sending a shiver down my spine.

"Excuse me, ladies," another voice says, and Sam whips around, facing them.

Please, not tonight.

"We're first," she snaps, placing her hands on her hips.

"Oh, I apologise," he says, humour in his tone.

Sam scoffs before rolling her eyes and turning back to Jake. "Look, we just want to go inside, sink some tequilas, and enjoy our bloody night."

"Maybe I could buy you a drink?" the guy behind us offers.

Sam whips around, pointing her finger at his chest. "Listen here. If you think you can offer to buy me a drink and I'm going to lie down and say yes, then you are one hundred percent correct."

A laugh rips through him as I pinch the bridge of my nose.

Turning on my heel to defuse the situation, I stumble as it catches in the drain, and everything happens in slow motion.

I brace myself for the impact of the concrete, but it never comes.

Strong hands jolt out and steady me, pulling me flush against a hard chest. I gasp, dragging my eyes up to meet theirs. Blue to *blue*.

His head tilts to the side as his eyes narrow on mine.

"Come on, Nico. Everyone's waiting for us." His friend clears his throat, breaking me from my trance.

Nico.

It suits him.

He gives his head a subtle shake before he releases my arms hesitantly, and I take a big step back.

"Careful," he says in a husky voice. I look down, breaking eye contact.

"Nico," his friend calls, louder this time.

"Coming," he bites out.

I watch as his perfectly polished shoes disappear, and I steal a glance, our eyes locking for a split second before the door shuts.

"So, before we were rudely interrupted ..." Sam turns her attention to Jake once again, and I turn to face them. "You were about to let us in."

"What's the name?" Jake says, rolling his eyes.

"Sam, Chloe, and Isabella."

The tip of his finger glides down the tablet before he finds our names. "There you are." He ticks us off before stepping back, nodding to his friend, who opens the wooden doors. "Enjoy your night, ladies."

"Jackass," Sam mumbles.

Once inside, we round the corridor, a glass banister in front of us. Our hands grasp the top as we look at the people on the floor below, getting lost in the music. The air smells expensive, a blend of sandalwood, amber, and orange from everyone's perfumes and colognes, leaving a sweetness in its wake, a hint of cigar hidden underneath.

Dancing poles are scattered around the corners of the rooms, beautiful women in gorgeous dresses clinging elegantly to them. I wish I could be like them, carefree, confident, and sexy, but I'm the complete opposite.

I glance down at my black dress, suddenly hit by self-consciousness.

"Come on," Chloe shouts over her shoulder as she heads down the stairs.

Sam and I follow closely.

My eyes catch the mirrors on every wall, the lighting from the crystal chandeliers bouncing off them. I'm not used to places like this; the ones we frequent have considerably less security and fights breaking out more often than not.

"Hello, ladies," the barman says as we reach him. "Welcome to Death by Kiss. What can I get you tonight?"

"Hey, cutie," Sam says as she leans against the bar, the lights flickering a sea of colours over her vibrant pink dress. "Is Beth here?"

The moment the words leave her mouth, we spot her at the far end of the bar, reaching for a bottle of wine.

"Bethy?!" the barman shouts, gaining her attention.

She smiles as she notices us. "Girls!" She blows us all a kiss, her chocolate-brown curls clipped neatly on top of her head. "You got in here ok, then?"

"Just about," I mumble to myself.

Chloe sniggers next to me.

"There was a little trouble, but nothing I couldn't handle," Sam says.

"Do I want to know?" Beth chuckles.

I shake my head.

With Sam, there's always a story.

"Aren't you going to introduce me?" the barman asks, throwing a tattooed arm over Beth's shoulder.

"Jax, these are my friends—Sam, Chloe, and Bella." She smiles at us. "Girls, this here is Jax—the biggest flirt on this side of London."

"I'm sorry, Bethy," Jax says, "but you hold that crown." He gives her a wink, and she flushes.

So this is the famous Jax we've been hearing so much about. Beth has mentioned that they have been flirting constantly for a while now, but it hasn't gone further, even though she wants to. Jax always stops it, and she doesn't know why.

"I beg to differ." She chuckles. "I think half the customers here know what colour your bedroom is." She masks the sting in her voice well.

Jax frowns and opens his mouth to reply, but Beth interrupts him.

"Right, ladies, I'm glad you're finally here. But it's my night in the VIP section, and those tips I'm not passing up on." She shrugs off Jax's arm and grabs two bottles of whiskey from the top shelf. "If you're still here when I clock off, maybe we can have a drink?"

"Oh, we'll still be here," Sam answers as she disappears down the bar.

Jax watches her before turning his attention to us. "So, my beautiful trio. What are we having?"

"Three tequilas to start, and then three strawberry daiquiris?"

"Coming right up." He rushes down the bar and gets to work on our order, his broad back straining against his white shirt as he reaches for the bottles.

"Tequila, really?" I shake my head. It's a recipe for me making a fool of myself.

Sam winks. "I just want you to loosen up a little, that's all." She squeezes my arm. "I want you to find someone tonight."

"If it hasn't happened in two years, it isn't going to." I wave her off.

"That's because you relegate everyone to the friend zone."

"I do not!" I bite back.

She and Chloe exchange a look.

"Babe, it's fine ... it's what you do. But you're young, and you need to get out there and enjoy life before you're a seventy-year-old woman feeding her nineteen cats and wishing she'd once had a fondle in the nightclub toilet."

I roll my eyes, but maybe she does have a point. "Fine!" I let out a frustrated breath. "If I find someone cute tonight, I promise you I'll at least think about asking for their number. But no toilet fondling."

"Hmm." Sam purses her lips. "How about we play a little game?"

"What kind of game?" I ask, raising my eyebrow.

"Not tonight," Chloe grumbles next to me as she sips her cocktail. "Can't we just have one night out where we don't make fools of ourselves?"

"Shush," Sam mutters to her, before a smile covers her whole face. "Let's see who can get the most numbers."

I shake my head. *This is a terrible idea.*

"Come on," Sam says, squeezing my hand. "It's just a little fun. Consider it practice—it will help build the confidence you need."

I grab a shot of tequila from the tray Jax deposits next to us. "Fine, but I'm going to need a hell of a lot of these." I gulp it down, the liquid burning my throat.

Sam smiles as she holds up her hand to Jax to order another round.

"The men here are high-end, as well," she says, her eyes dancing around the room.

She isn't wrong.

I run my hands uncertainly down my dress.

"Exactly. Look at them. They aren't going to be interested in someone who waits tables for a living."

"Babe, don't sell yourself short. We *all* wait tables for a living," Chloe offers. "You are beautiful, clever, and your personality is unmatched. So, pull up your Bridget Jones knickers and let's all pretend we're someone else for the night."

"Yes!" Sam says a little too loudly, gaining people's attention. "I'm now known as Hannah. I'm an accountant from the States. Nice to meet you," she says in an American accent as she sends us a wink. "See you on the flip side, baby," she adds as she downs her second shot and disappears into the crowd.

Chapter 2

Dominic

"Bro, quit staring, it's creepy as shit," Joey says, nudging me to draw my attention away from the cute blonde that captured my attention outside.

"I'm not staring," I snap, but it's a lie.

I couldn't pull my eyes away even if I wanted to.

"Ok ..." He drawls out the word as he takes a sip of his whiskey, his eyes landing back onto the dance floor, where she weaves in and out of people. Her black dress sways with her steps, revealing more of her toned legs. "She is hot."

He holds up his hands in surrender at my glare. "Is she playing some sort of game?" he asks as he leans forward in his chair, his eyes zoning in on her.

"Could be." We watch as she weaves her way through the crowd. She strolls up to numerous guys, chatting with them for a few minutes before shaking her head at her friends, who watch from the bar, before moving on to the next.

I can't help but be intrigued.

"Right, enough of this," Joey says, slapping me on the leg as he stands. "I have my own pretty blonde giving me the eye," he adds before disappearing into the crowd.

I roll my eyes. Joey can't help himself; he sees a pretty woman and he's putty in their hands.

"Everything ok, Nico?" Nancy places a slender, manicured hand on my thigh as she drops down next to me in Joey's vacant seat.

My eyes flick down to the contact, and I don't even try to hide my frown.

"Everything's fine, Nancy. Why don't you join in with the celebrations?"

We received another innocent verdict today, which, as per Joey's rules, is why we're out to celebrate.

"I'd much rather spend my time with you," she says in a low, seductive tone.

Normally, I might take her up on her offer, but tonight my attentions are elsewhere.

I ignore her, my eyes flicking back to the dance floor, but in the brief moment of distraction, I've lost sight of her.

I take a sip of my whiskey, and the liquid slips easily down my throat.

"You sure I can't help you loosen up?" Nancy pushes, and I shake my head.

"Not interested."

"Sometimes you can be a right asshole," she snaps, shooting to her feet and storming off.

I lean forward in my chair, placing my glass down on the table in front of me.

There she is.

I don't know what game she's playing, but it's my turn.

I push my way through the crowd, a lion stalking its prey, eyes focused solely on her. I watch as she shakes her head at her friends again, not bothering to look where she's going—so naturally, she bumps hard, face-first into my chest, those ridiculously high heels of hers making her stumble.

Again.

My hands jolt out instinctively, grasping her upper arms and steadying her.

Again.

"Oh shit." She gasps, her face buried into my chest for a second before she steps back, my hands falling from her.

Recognition hits. "You?" she says before her eyes flick down and widen. "Oh my God, I'm so sorry!"

I follow her eyeline and notice the droplets of her strawberry daiquiri on my crisp white shirt.

She uses her fingertips to try and brush it off, but it only makes it worse, seeping further into the material

"It's fine," I say, and she steps back.

"You really need to get that soaked before it's wrecked completely."

I smile at her concern, but I have hundreds of white shirts at home.

"I've been watching you."

I slam my mouth shut. Creepy was not the vibe I was going for.

She arches her eyebrow.

"Err, what I mean by that—"

"Oh yes, I can't wait to hear you speak your way out of this one," she says dryly, crossing her arms and trying to suppress a smile.

"What I mean is that I recognised you from outside and wondered whether you knew all of the people you've spoken to tonight."

"I mean, not really," she says, shrugging.

"Not really?" My brows pinch together.

How can you 'not really' know people?

"God." She pinches the bridge of her nose for a second before shaking out her shoulders and standing straight. "My friend said I suck at flirting, so we're playing a little game ..."

Joey was right.

"Who could get the most guys' numbers by the end of the night." She chuckles softly, her cheeks flushed. "Sounds silly when you say it out loud."

"Tell me," I say, taking a small step closer. "Are you winning?"

She shakes her head, and I watch her visibly swallow.

My lips tug into a smile as the air around us thickens.

"Shame."

She looks away from me, her eyes searching the crowd of people dancing around us.

I'm losing her ... and I'm not ready for that yet.

"Try flirting with me," I offer.

Her mouth opens and closes a few times. "You ... want me to flirt with you?" The uncertainty is firmly back on her face, and I don't like it.

I straighten the sleeve of my blazer, distracting myself from reaching out and pulling her flush against me.

"Yes."

She shakes her head. "I couldn't."

"Why not?"

"I mean, I could?" She thinks about it for a second. "Ok, fuck it." She smiles widely. "What can I lose? Nothing." She shakes her body out, as if she's psyching herself up for something serious.

It makes me smile.

"I'm Isabella, but you can call me Bel. Bella." She doesn't even stop for a breath. "I mean, sometimes my friends call me Panda, as a joke, because I'm clumsy.

This year they bought me a panda teddy ... oh, wait. What's your name?"

"Dominic."

"Short and sweet," she says, her face lighting up. "Maybe I should be more like you, Dom."

Dom. I like it.

"You wouldn't want to be like me, Shortcake." The words are out of my mouth before I have a chance to stop them.

"Why not? You seem pretty put together. Strawberry daiquiri excluded." Her eyes drop down my body before she gives her head a subtle shake. They land firmly back on my face and hold.

She's good at eye contact.

My mouth opens and closes a few times. I'm never one for a loss for words.

"I'm a workaholic."

"Workaholic?" She grimaces. "That's not good, Dom. When do you get time for yourself?"

"Time for myself?" In thirty years, I've never had time to myself. Maybe when I was in nappies, but I can imagine that then, I was planning my next bottle.

"This isn't flirting." She chuckles, slapping my hand. "So, tell me, Dom, do you come here often?" she says in a low, seductive tone.

A laugh rips through me.

She smiles widely.

"Mainly for business."

"Business, hey?" She steps closer, lowering her voice. "Is it top secret?"

I nod.

"You work for the police, don't you?" She gives me a look, and I leave her question hanging in the air. "Let me guess ..." She taps her finger against her lips as she thinks before pointing at me. "Detective?"

I arch my eyebrow.

"No! Wait!" she says loudly, gaining a couple of guys' attention next to us. I shoot them a look, and they avert their gazes. "You're undercover, aren't you?" She says it seriously before bursting into a fit of giggles.

A snort leaves her lips, and she blushes.

She's cute.

"Anyway, thanks for this, Dom," she says. "I needed it. I think I can now go out there and, who knows ..." She holds her arms wide. "Maybe flirt up a storm? See you around."

She spins on her heels.

"Wait," I say, and she freezes, looking over her shoulder at me. "You forgot to ask for my number."

She pauses for a second, her brows pinching.

"I'll see you around, Dom," she says before disappearing into the crowd.

Chapter 3

Isabella

We fall through our front door the moment we manage to open it.

Chloe pushes past us, stumbling over her own feet before landing in a heap on the sofa.

"Shit, how much did she drink?" Sam slurs, chuckling as she rips open the paper and stuffs her kebab into her mouth, mayonnaise dripping down her chin and landing on the floor. "Oopsie."

I chuckle along with her as I take a massive bite of my own, the deliciousness of it making me close my eyes for a second. There's nothing better than a greasy kebab after a night out.

My eyes snap to Chloe as she snores quietly. "Shall we wake her or save hers for tomorrow?"

Sam's head turns to her, a small smile tugging at her lips. "Let's save it for tomorrow ... because I don't know about you, but I don't think I have it in me to hold her hair back whilst she pukes."

A laugh rips through me as I take another bite, trying to stop the salad from falling out.

"Those dusty canvases"—Sam jerks her head to the corner of the living room—"shall we throw them in the trash? Or are you ever going to start painting again?"

I shoot her a look.

Over the last few months, I've been working on my art as much as I can in my spare time, but I've kept it to myself. I'm even starting a class this coming week to perfect my technique.

"I'll take that as a no," Sam mutters as she drops her kebab onto the kitchen side and rushes towards my canvases, pulling one from behind the curtains.

"Don't you dare!" I screech as I dart towards her, my hands wrapping around the canvas and tugging it towards me, but she doesn't release it. "Gimme!"

"Why should I?" She raises her eyebrow, challenging me.

"Because ..." I stutter, my tongue darting out and wetting my dry lips. "I'm not ready to get rid of them yet."

Her brows pull together as her face softens. "Babe, you need to live your life; Jason would want that."

"I know," I say, a lump in my throat.

She gives me a pointed look, letting out a deep sigh, but chooses to drop it. “God, I’m going to be so hungover in the morning.”

“Yes, you are,” I say, chuckling. “It’s all the drinks you were tricking people into buying us.”

“What?!” she says as she takes another bite. “Those prices were going to cripple me. If I can flirt my way into free drinks, then babe, I’m going to do it.”

I laugh, because she is right. As beautiful as the club was, we probably wouldn’t go back. The prices for cocktails alone were extortionate.

Chloe's snore rips through the air. “I think we need to carry her to bed. There's no way we can leave her on there ... do you remember the last time?”

“God, do I ever,” Sam says, sighing. “We didn’t stop hearing about it for a week.”

“Come on.” I make my way towards Chloe, who's sprawled out on the sofa. There’s a little dribble in the corner of her mouth as I reach under her arms. Sam copies me as she grabs her legs.

“Oh my God, she’s a dead weight.” Sam moans as we weave our way through the mismatched furniture and head into Chloe's room. The moment we flick on the light, we’re blinded by the crystals that sparkle from it. Her whole bedroom is made up of things from charity shops, furniture she has remodelled herself.

We drop her into the middle of the bed as Sam covers her in a blanket.

"Does she look comfortable to you?" she asks, her head tilted to the side.

Does she look comfortable? Is she taking the piss? Her legs are hanging off the end of the bed, and her neck is at a forty-five-degree angle.

"Yeah, she sure does," I say as we back out of the room and I flick off the light, shutting her door. "I guess we'd better hit the hay, too?"

"Yup," Sam says as she reaches into her pocket and pulls out a bag of Maltesers. "Night, babe!"

"When I said use these canvases, I didn't mean at three am." Sam yawns as she leans against my door-frame. Her once light pink pyjamas now have stains on them, but she refuses to throw them away.

"Sorry, I couldn't help myself," I say, rolling my aching shoulders. All the alcohol from tonight has finally worn off after drinking three boiling cups of tea, eating that dirty kebab, and having an ice-cold shower. "I think I managed an hour or two of sleep, but then the need to paint became too much."

"Bel," she says, rubbing her eyes and letting out a yawn. Guilt rips through me.

"I'm sorry if I woke you," I say, twisting in my chair and facing her as I wipe the paint on my apron.

"It's fine; it's my day off tomorrow, anyway." Her eyes land on my hidden pile in the corner.

"What's that?" Sam darts towards them, pulling back the blanket and revealing my art. Each is different from the last.

"Sam," I mumble.

"Wow, babe." She gasps as she flicks through them. "These are fucking amazing! When did you start painting again? And why didn't you tell me?"

"Thanks," I say. Heat rushes to my cheeks. "Because I didn't want people to see any of my pieces until I was happy with them."

"You know ..." she muses as she turns to face me, and I see the look of determination written across her face. "You nearly have enough here for your own exhibition."

I shake my head, dismissing the idea.

It doesn't mean I haven't been thinking about it, dreaming about it, but the prospect of actually going ahead with it makes me instantly feel sick.

"Don't dismiss anything yet, babe," she says as she stops right in front of me. "Think about it. I can help you."

"I don't know how."

"Babe, it's me we're talking about. There's always a way." She scoffs as she places her hands on her hips. "You know, you could hold it at Wilson's. There's no way Phoebe and Manny would charge you. You're like a daughter to them."

I shake my head. I couldn't ask them to close down the restaurant for me—not at their busiest time of day.

"Stop thinking of others and start thinking of yourself. This could be everything for you. You've always wanted your art in galleries." She wraps her arm over my shoulder as she pushes me across my bench and settles in next to me. "If I promote this for you, who knows who will come. You could actually be picked up ..."

I tune her out as I let her words sink in.

Is she right?

Is it finally time to give this my whole heart?

"What do you say?" she asks, her eyes on mine. "Come on, you know I can do it."

In my opinion, Sam has the potential to be the best party planner in London.

I finally nod.

"EEK! I'm so excited." She screams in excitement, and I shush her, clamping my hand over her mouth.

"Shush! Chloe's fast asleep."

Chapter 4

Isabella - Age 13

"Isabella?" Miss Norris, my art teacher, calls after me as I and all the other students rush out of the class, ready to head home.

I pause, turning to face her as people push past.

"Can I have a moment, please?" she asks, and my shoulders drop as I let out a deep breath.

"I was thinking about your artwork." She has my full attention now. There's nothing better than having a paintbrush in my hands and letting my imagination come to life. "Now, Isabella, you have a real natural talent ... it's beyond anything I've ever seen before."

The heat rises to my cheeks as she continues.

"But you need more practice," she says as she perches herself on the end of her desk. "Is this something you can do at home?"

I shake my head, my eyes dropping to my feet. The school isn't stupid; they realised quite quickly that we didn't have money.

Jason has been saving up to buy me paints and brushes, but I told him not to bother. Food and clothes are more important.

"Hmm," she mutters as she taps her finger against her lips. "What about if I give you the equipment?"

My eyes snap to hers, and I shake my head. "I couldn't afford to pay, Miss."

"I don't want any money," she blurts out in alarm, pushing off the desk and heading to the locked cupboard at the back. None of the students have ever been in here, and we've always wondered what it's for.

So far, the rumours have included a dead body.

I'm not going to burst their bubble.

"Wow," I say as I walk further into the cupboard, my eyes flickering everywhere.

"Right, you're going to need one of these." She grabs a packet of different-sized paintbrushes and drops them into my arms.

"Oomph," I mumble.

She sighs as she places her hands on her hips for a second. "We're going to need a box."

"A box?"

"Yes, to hold all of this," she says, waving her hands in front of her as she grabs a big box, shoving small canvases inside.

"Miss, I can't take all of this," I say, sadness washing over me.

I want nothing more than to be able to, to work on my paintings from home—and who knows, maybe one day have my work in galleries ... but things like that never happen for people like me.

"Shh, now." She cuts me off. "This is my gift to you. The school won't notice it's gone. And when you make it, you remember me."

Unlocking the front door, I pause and listen for my parents. Silence.

My breath leaves me as my shoulders relax, and I head inside and rush to my room, kicking the door shut behind me. I place the box on the floor.

Miss Noris has always been my favourite teacher.

She's quirky and unique. Her dark brown hair is always piled on top of her head, with a bright red bandana and paintbrushes sticking out. She's funny and doesn't care for the teachers' rules. She swears a lot and always tells us to throw our emotions onto the canvas.

That's where I've found my calling: landscape. I love painting places; even if I have never been to a place before, I can paint what is in my imagination, or what I have seen in books.

"Isab—" My mother barges into my room unannounced, and her voice cuts off. She glances at the box in front of me.

I stumble, gathering everything I can and shoving it back inside the box, kicking it behind me. "Mum." I try to hide my panic, but I know I fail. "I didn't realise you were home."

"What do you have there?" She tries to look behind me, but I take a step to the side, blocking her view.

"Nothing."

"Isabella, I'm not stupid. Move." She pushes me out of the way as she bends down, rummaging through the box. "All of this must have cost a fair bit. Where did you get it?"

"From school."

I stand awkwardly behind her, hoping, praying that she leaves soon and forgets about this.

"You're telling me that the school just handed this over ... for free?" she says as she pushes off her knees and stands up straight. Her face doesn't hide the accusation.

Does she think I stole this?

I nod, hoping she believes me and leaves this alone.

"Right ..." She draws out the word as she turns. "Well, it's time for dinner."

I follow her into the kitchen, and Jason pulls out the chair next to him for me, ruffling my hair as I drop into it.

"Alright, squirt?" Jason says as he tucks into beans on toast.

"So, that art stuff ..." my mother immediately begins before I even have a chance to have my first mouthful. My eyes snap to hers.

Is she really bringing it up in the middle of dinner?

I feel my parents' eyes boring into my face.

"Your teacher *gave* it to you? Why?"

I shrug. "Maybe because she sees something in me," I say quietly.

"Isabella ..." My dad sighs. "What have I told you? We don't have time or the money for this. It's an expensive hobby."

Jason's leg nudges mine under the table. His knuckles whiten as he grips his knife and fork tightly.

I give my head a subtle shake.

As much as he likes to protect me, I need him to keep his mouth closed right now.

The rest of the meal is finished in silence before I head back to my room, throwing myself down onto the bed.

Is it my parents' life mission to make sure I can never be happy?

Between their drinking, gambling, and pushing my brother out to get a job before he was ready, I can't remember the last time I was truly happy.

The door to my bedroom opens and Jason sneaks in, dropping down next to me on the bed and tugging me towards him. "Ignore them, squirt." He pauses as he scratches his chin. "We will find the money, somehow."

I remain silent, staring at the cracks on my bedroom ceiling, silence filling the air.

"You know, one day we will get out of here, start again," he says quietly as I rest my head on his shoulder.

God, I hope so.

He pauses as he reaches into his jeans pocket, before holding out a silver bracelet. "I got you this."

Sitting up, I take it off him. It's beautiful, with different London-related charms dangling from it.

Big Ben.

The London Eye.

A bright red bus.

"Jase, where did you get this?" I smile, tears glistening in my eyes. My hand strokes every single little charm. It's beautiful.

"I saw it in the shop I pass every day to work." He smiles as he takes the bracelet from me and fastens it around my wrist. The charms clink together as I admire them. "And I wanted to get it for you, as a promise that one day I will take you to London, and we'll start again."

Chapter 5

Isabella

Jason,

I got my first tattoo; it's only a small one. A little star on my left ankle. It wasn't planned, but we got drunk and somehow I woke up with it. You should see what Sam got ...

I'm starting an art class soon. I'm really looking forward to it, and I can't wait for you to finally get to see me paint again.

I love you <3

Where are my ... "Gotcha!"

This is the fourth time this week, and it's Friday.

"Keys in the fridge again?" Sam asks from the sofa.

"Yup," I say as I close the fridge behind me, grabbing my cold cup of juice from the side.

I'm already fifteen minutes late for my shift downstairs as I spent most of last night painting. I have huge bags under my eyes, and my hair is worse than ever, but I don't have time to do anything about it.

"I bought you that key finder for Christmas, and you never use it." Sam shakes her head as she shovels her spoon into the tub of ice cream she's devouring.

"I will, I will." I wave her off.

It's March, and I've still not even taken it out of the packaging.

"Oh, and Bel?" I pause. "You've got paint on your face."

I reach up, touching my cheek, and feel the dry paint. I scratch it off, not caring if it leaves a mark. I'm already late as it is.

"Argh, what a morning," Chloe says as she walks in from her shift downstairs.

I moved to London seven years ago—a naïve seventeen-year-old with only nine hundred pounds to my name. No job experience or anything. Thankfully, Phoebe and Manny, the owners of Wilson's, saw something in me. I think it was out of pity, but it doesn't matter, because they gave me a job, and that's where I met Sam and Chloe. The first shift, we hit it off. They offered me the spare room in the flat upstairs, and we've been friends ever since.

"Hey, babe." I press a kiss to her cheek as I pass, grabbing my bag off the hook. "Is it busy down there?"

"Oh yes." She kicks off her shoes before dropping herself onto the sofa next to Sam with a groan. "It doesn't help that this one kept plying us with tequila last night."

"Don't blame me." Sam shrugs off her comments. "You could have said no."

"Oh yeah, because you would have listened." Chloe scoffs.

Sam holds out the ice cream, and Chloe grabs it gladly, shovelling it into her mouth.

"Speaking of last night ..." Chloe mumbles between mouthfuls. "You were on fire!"

Fire's one word for it.

I'd say disaster.

"That one guy you were talking to ..." She fans herself with her hands. "Now he was hot!"

"He was ok."

"What's wrong? I can hear your brain working from here," Sam asks as she snatches the ice cream back from Chloe.

"Nothing."

She gives me a pointed look.

"Seriously, nothing." I laugh it off. "I just realised last night that my flirting game isn't what it should be."

My flirting game isn't just what it should be; it's non-existent. I mean, who at twenty-four googles how to flirt? *Me, that's who.* It's embarrassing, to say the least.

"You're just learning this now?" Sam's brow rises. "You've been out of the game for a while, but it's just to get back onto the horse ... and if you happen to ride a cowboy or two, then so be it." She shrugs.

"Shit, I need to go!"

"Good morning, beautiful." Phoebe blows me a kiss as I place my things in my locker. "It's been one hell of a morning." She takes off her shoes and rubs her feet.

Phoebe isn't your normal fifty-year-old. She's adventurous, daring, and could drink anyone under the table.

"Why don't you go home, honey?" Manny says as he wipes his hands on the towel, his worried eyes focusing on his wife. She broke her foot a few weeks ago when she fell in the kitchen, but that never stopped her.

She dismisses the idea straight away. "We're still busy; you need me."

"We don't need you," he says, shaking his head. "Bella is here now." He gives me a look for me to back him up.

"Only if you're sure?" She looks up, her eyes on mine, and I nod. "Thank you both," she says, putting her shoes back on and kissing Manny before leaving.

"Thanks, Bel," Manny says, letting out a breath. "She isn't ready to be back at work, but you know what she's like."

"I do." I rub his shoulder reassuringly. "But I'm here now; let's do this."

The smell of fresh coffee hits me, and the aroma of fried breakfast fills the air as I rush to help Angel and Georgina, wiping down the oak tables. Fairy lights wrap around exposed wooden beams, illuminating some of my old paintings on the walls. My eyes drift over the soft strokes of the ocean and the bright colours of Phoebe's garden.

"Hey girls," I say, smiling.

"I'm so glad the rush has died down; my feet are killing me," Georgina says as she shakes out her feet. My eyes drop to her bright pink diamanté sandals.

"I don't blame them."

She frowns. "I know it's my fault; I forgot my black pumps. Anyway, how was last night?"

"It was ..." I pause, thinking of the right word. "Unexpected."

"Unexpected?" Her brows pinch together.

I've been kicking myself ever since I declined Dom's request for my number, but that's how I met my ex, Myles—on the dance floor. He came sliding up next to me, trying to impress me with his moves. Sadly, it didn't work, but his charm did. He made me laugh, and we exchanged numbers, and the rest was history. Until one day two years ago when I walked in on him balls-deep in a redhead. I think I stood there for all of a minute before my brain kicked into gear and I grabbed the nearest thing I could and launched it at his head.

Since then, I've promised myself I wouldn't make the same mistake. Now I have a brick wall built up higher than the estate building around my heart, and it's going to take more than a sledgehammer to knock it down.

"I met someone," I say, leaning my hip against the table, playing with the cloth in my hand.

Angel's eyes light up as she takes a seat. "Who?! Tell me all."

"Well, his name is Dominic. Dominic Barone, I think the doorman said." Gee's eyes focus on mine, something flickering in them. "He spotted me acting silly, trying my hand at flirting." I shake my head at that—I should have called it a night when the first guy asked me if I shaved my toes. I mean, I might, but that's not something I will be broadcasting to the world. "And he asked me to try with him."

Georgina remains quiet.

"He asked you to flirt with him?" Angel gushes. She's a complete bookaholic and such a sucker for a love story.

"Oh, yeah." I shake my head, remembering my failed attempt. "I think it's safe to say that flirting and I don't mix."

"You just need practice," Georgina says. Her eyes focus behind me and widen. "I ... I need to speak to Manny about something," she rushes out before disappearing.

Angel frowns, and I shrug.

"Good morning, Shortcake," a deep voice says, and I whip around.

It's Dominic. At ... Wilson's?

He looks so perfect for the morning—compared to me.

His perfect navy suit is in place, and his crisp white shirt looks as if it were freshly pressed this morning.

A smile threatens to spill as I picture him making sure every single crease is out.

Angel nudges me.

Last night, Chloe had worked her magic on me, but right now I have the smallest amount of mascara on, my hair is piled in a messy bun on top of my head, with all the pieces sticking out everywhere, and I'm in my work uniform. Yes, it's a white shirt and a black skirt, but still, it's no comparison to my little black dress.

"Uh ... hi," I mumble back quietly, my confidence from last night gone.

I need some more tequila.

"How are you feeling this morning?" he asks.

Angel's eyes burn into the side of my head as she stands next to me.

"I'm fine, thanks." It comes out sharper than intended.

I don't mean to be short, but having him here, in my personal space, is knocking me off kilter. I never expected to see him again, yet here he is.

"I'm sorry, but my friend here seems to have forgotten her manners." Angel cuts her eyes to me before smiling sweetly at Dominic. "I'm Angel, Isabella's friend."

Dominic's eyes flick to mine before he turns his attention to Angel, a professional smile in place. "Hello, I'm Dominic." He holds out his hand for her to shake.

Powerful and professional ... I wonder if this is how he is at work?

The idea of him telling me what to do rushes to my mind, and my cheeks flush.

Dominic's eyes drop to my reddened cheeks, and his lips turn up in a smile.

"Aren't you going to show Dominic to his table?" Angel prompts me.

I cut my eyes to her.

Why can't you do it? I want to scream, but instead I settle for sending her a look.

She smiles sweetly at me, spinning me around and giving me a light nudge.

Bitch. I need to remember to pay her back for this.

"If you'd like to follow me," I say tightly, grabbing a menu and walking through the restaurant, passing the crowds of people that have started to pile in for the lunch rush. I feel him close on my heel, but don't turn around until we reach his table. I motion for him to take a seat.

"Thanks, Shortcake."

"Here." I pass him the menu. "I'll give you a few minutes, and I'll be back to take your order."

I take a step, but his voice halts me.

"What do you recommend?"

"It depends. I'm a fussy eater," I say, shrugging.

He smiles, his eyes flicking down to the menu before he holds it out to me. "I'll take a ham salad sandwich and a Coke."

Good choice.

Retrieving the menu from him, I make my way back to Angel and slam it onto the counter. "Why did you do that?!"

She smirks. "Because"—she lowers her voice as she leans over the counter, her face close to mine—"it's clear to anyone that guy over there is into you, and it seems you need a nudge in the right direction before you friend-zone him like everybody else."

My face falls as I stand up straight. "I-I—"

"It's not your fault, Bel. It's a defence mechanism. But you have to stop now and give this guy a chance. He seems ... nice." She tilts her head as she looks behind me, and her eyes soften.

I glance over my shoulder, and my eyes clash with Dominic's.

Butterflies riot in my stomach.

“Bella! Order for table five.” Manny cuts me out of my daze as I throw the cloth into the sink.

“Thanks,” I say, grabbing Dominic’s order.

My feet drag as I make my way over to him, his head buried in his phone.

I place the plate down in front of him with a little more force than necessary, and the top of his sandwich falls off.

“Thanks, Shortcake,” he says, his eyes meeting mine as he tucks his phone into his pocket.

My hands tremble slightly at the weight of his stare.

“Ok, well, enjoy,” I rush out as I turn around, ready to high-tail it out of here.

“Can I ask you a question before you scurry off again?” he says. I turn back and frown.

“I didn’t scurry.”

“Could’ve fooled me,” he says, amusement in his eyes. “We can argue about that if you’d like, but you’re clearly busy, and I'd rather take the time to ask you my question." His perfect white teeth show as he smiles.

I place my hand on my hip as I raise my eyebrow, waiting.

"Why wouldn't you give me your number?"

My mouth opens and closes as I think of an answer.

"Because ..." I stutter. "I ..."

"I'm not hearing a reason," he says, pulling out his phone and handing it to me.

I reach out to take it from him, our fingertips graze, and I freeze.

A spark shoots through me.

Does he feel it too?

I type in my number and hand the phone back to him—before this time actually scurrying away.

Chapter 6

Isabella

"Hello, Isabella," Frankie, the art teacher, says as I enter the room. The smell of paint instantly hits me, and my shoulders relax. "It's nice to put a face to the voice, and you have a very symmetrical face." A laugh slips past my lips. "Now, if you could place your things on the hooks, we will begin shortly." She strides to the front of the room, her green dress swaying with every step.

I make my way towards the hooks, my eyes drawn to the vibrant colours on the walls. People give me warm smiles as I pass and hang my coat on a spare hook.

"Hey," a deep voice says. I turn to face the owner, my eyes landing on a young guy. His blue eyes meet mine, and I smile. "I'm Ollie."

“Isabella,” I reply quietly as he shrugs off his coat and falls into step with me until I find an empty seat.

“Nice to meet you, Bella,” he says, brushing back his blonde hair that’s fallen in front of his eyes. After placing his phone into his beige cargo trousers, he takes the seat next to mine.

“Welcome, everyone,” Frankie begins, gaining everyone's attention. “Now, as you can all see, we have a new face today. Welcome, Bella.” Her smile is directed at me, and I return it. “Now today, we are painting the ocean ... the beautiful colours of the waves lapping gloriously against the sand.” She picks up an acrylic paintbrush and dabs it into the orange paint, smearing it along the blank canvas. “As we all know, starting with a bright colour first will bring the richness of the tones together.”

She turns to face us. “Now, please, begin.” She nods, and everyone starts immediately.

“If you need any help, Bella,” Ollie says next to me, drawing my attention to him, “just let me know.”

I smile. “Thanks.”

I pick up the paintbrush and dip it into the bright colours. The moment my brush touches the blank canvas, I get lost in the piece, a warmth rushing through me.

“Well done, Isabella. Remember, art is supposed to be fun. It isn’t about just what you see in front of you, but it's about what you see inside,” she says as she presses her hand against her heart. "We need to work on bringing out the emotion, the spark."

"Bella!" I jump, jolted out of my trance. "Time's up," Ollie adds, and my eyes snap towards the clock. Shit, class is over.

"Well done, Bella," Frankie says as her eyes land on my canvas. They light up as she takes in every line and detail. "But please, remember to allow yourself to let go when painting."

"I will."

"You have real talent," she adds, pressing her hand on my shoulder.

"Thank you," I say with a smile.

"I will see you both next Thursday." She gives me one final look before she spins on her heel and leaves us alone.

"Well done, Bella," Ollie says as he grabs his bag and throws it over his shoulder. "I was thinking ... do you fancy grabbing a drink?"

My eyes snap to his.

"Hey ..." He holds his hands up in the air. "We'll be sitting next to each other every week now, so I think we need to make sure neither of us are psychos."

A chuckle slips past my lips. "Ok, fine. What did you have in mind?"

"What shall we do?"

"Let's grab a drink. I know a place," I say, and he nods eagerly as he falls into step with me.

"I can't believe this is your favourite." Ollie scoffs, humour in his tone. We had a drink at Wilson's after class, and because the night is still young, we decided to opt for watching a movie back at the flat.

"Why?" I ask incredulously, the opening credits to *Bridget Jones's Diary* playing.

It's unbeatable.

Mr. Darcy and Daniel Cleaver are both dreamboats, and I'd like to meet anyone who says otherwise.

He forces out a laugh. "It's just that these kinds of films are completely unrealistic. They give females false expectations."

My brows pinch together. "It's just a romance. It's fiction; it's not real."

"How about ..." He pauses as he scratches his chin. "*500 Days of Summer*?"

"Never seen it," I say with a shrug as we both reach for the remote at the same time. His hand covers mine, and I instantly snatch mine back.

A frown tugs at his brows.

"Did you see his face?" Sam's laugh echoes off the walls as the door bursts open—and relief washes through me.

"Yeah, because you dropped that whole mug of tea onto his lap," Chloe adds.

"It was an accid—" Sam's words die in her mouth as they both turn and spot us.

I send them a smile, but they don't return it.

"Hi, ladies," Ollie says next to me, his arm draping behind me on the sofa.

"Oh, hello," Sam says, her eyes flicking between us. "I didn't realise you had company." She directs the last bit at me.

Chloe motions her head in my direction to follow them.

“I'll be right back,” I say to Ollie, and I dart out of the living room after them.

As soon as I enter the kitchen, their heads whip in my direction as they both lean on the counter.

“What?”

“Who’s that?” Sam asks first. “A new boyfriend?”

I roll my eyes. “His name is Ollie. I met him at art class earlier.”

“He looks ... nice,” Chloe teases. “Shall we get our bridesmaids' dresses fitted now, or later?”

“Shut up.” I chuckle, gently shoving her arm.

“I’m joking,” she says, holding her hands up in surrender. “It’s the first time you’ve ever bought a guy home. What are we supposed to think?”

“It’s true, we thought you were turning into a nun or something,” Sam adds.

I shrug. “He’s just a friend.”

They exchange a look.

“A friend with benefits or an actual friend?” Sam asks.

“An actual friend.”

“Ok ...” She draws out the word and plates up her food, grabbing herself a Coke from the fridge. “Come on, he must be wondering what we’re up to in here,” she adds, grabbing her things and disappearing back into the living room.

“Let's go save your *friend* before Sam interrogates him,” Chloe says.

Sure enough, Sam has taken my vacant seat as we head back in.

"Come sit next to me, babe." Chloe pats the seat next to her. She covers us in a blanket as I feel the weight of Ollie's stare.

I give him a small smile as Sam presses play and the TV roars to life.

"So, Ollie ... tell me about you?"

"What about me?"

"Do you work?"

He nods. "I work in IT."

"That's good. Do you have your own place?"

"I do."

Talk about interrogation ...

"What about a special person in your life?"

"Sam," I warn, shooting her a look to quit, but she ignores me.

"It's fine, Bella," Ollie says, his eyes softening on mine. "No, I'm single."

"That's a shame," Sam says between bites. "Maybe we should sign you up to a dating app. I'm sure you'll be snapped right up."

Ollie shrugs uncomfortably. "No, I've tried ... the apps are much easier for females."

"There are loads of women out there; maybe you need to broaden your radius."

"Sam," I say, shaking my head at her.

"It's fine, Bella," Ollie says to me before turning his attention back on Sam. "I've been on every site possible, I've gone out to nightclubs, bars, and still nothing. Girls don't really go for guys like me. I'm not tall or wealthy enough."

Silence fills the air.

"Bella ... I need to go. Walk me to the door?"

I nod as I throw back the blanket and follow behind him. Sam shoots me a look as I pass.

Once we reach the door, he turns to face me.

"That was intense, huh?" I joke, trying to break the thick tension.

"It sure was," he says. Rolling his shoulders, he lets out a breath before his face softens, and he takes a step closer to me. "Listen, Bel, as much as your friends are great ..." He clears his throat as my brows pinch together. "That was all a bit much. We should do something just the two of us."

I nod weakly as he presses a kiss against my cheek. "Let's say Saturday? We can grab dinner."

"Perfect," I mumble as he gives me one final look before leaving.

Dragging my hands down my face, I inhale a deep breath.

Chapter 7

Isabella

Dominic: I think waiting over twenty-four hours to send a message is enough to stop a guy coming across too interested, no?

Me: I'm sorry, who is this?

Dominic: Funny, Shortcake.

Me: Funny? Me?

Dominic: Are you trying to flirt again? I think you need more practice. With me.

"Come on, we need to hurry, or we'll miss our reservation," Ollie says as he clasps my hand

and drags me down the street. I stumble slightly on my heels but manage to keep up with him.

He hasn't told me where we're going, so I've opted for casual but cute, wearing a black skater dress borrowed from Chloe and pairing it with black strappy heels.

Thank God for her, because without her, it would be jeans and a T-shirt.

"We're here," he says, letting out a breath as he pulls open the door to the restaurant, and I take a glance at the sign above.

Romano's.

Holy shit.

Why didn't he tell me he'd booked this place? There's no way I would have worn this.

"Here?" I hesitate as I look through the window.

"Yeah," he says, smiling. He pushes open the door, and I follow.

"Hey, reservation for the name Oliver Preston."

I clasp my hands around my bag for emotional support as my eyes drift over the open space.

Crisp white tablecloths are laid neatly over round, circular tables, with red plush velvet chairs that are fully occupied. Candles are lit on every table, accompanied by soft white fresh roses. Soft jazz music plays in the background, its hum blending with quiet chatter.

The waitress smiles, motioning with her head for us to follow.

"Someone will be over soon to take your order," she says as we take our seats. "In the meantime, can I get you any drinks?"

I go to open my mouth, but Ollie speaks first. "Yes, can we get two glasses of pinot grigio?"

I press my lips together as the waitress leaves.

Pinot grigio was always Mum's drink of choice.

"This place is fancy, huh?" He nudges my leg with his.

I nod, my shoulders dropping as I give the menu my full attention.

"What are you having?" he asks without looking up from his.

"I'm not sure," I say, playing with the charms on my bracelet. I'm not sure I want to spend a month's wages on a meal I probably won't enjoy.

"There's so much I fancy," he says. I look up, and my eyes meet his.

A waitress sidles up to the table, breaking his stare. "Have you decided, or would you like some more time?"

"I'll have the filet steak, medium rare, with sweet potato fries," Ollie says, closing the menu and holding it out to the waitress.

She takes it with a smile before turning her attention to me.

"Does the tomato soup come with bread?"

"It does." She smiles sweetly.

"I'll just have that then, please. As a main."

My shoulders relax slightly as I pass her the menu, and she departs for the kitchen.

"So," Ollie says, clasping his hands together on the table. "Tell me about your life. What have you been up to lately?"

"Not much," I reply quickly as I play with the petals on the rose. "We went to Soho the other night." A small chuckle slips past my lips as I remember how drunk we got. "It was really good fun. We danced, played a game—"

"What kind of game?"

"Um ... how many numbers we could get ..."

God, saying it out loud sounds a bit pathetic, but it wasn't at the time. I haven't laughed so much in a while.

His brows pinch together. "Don't you think that's a bit dangerous?"

My mouth slams shut.

"Some men might see that as a green light, and I would hate for you to put yourself into a position like that."

"It was just a little fun." I let out a nervous laugh. Is he right?

"I'm only saying it because I don't want you to get hurt."

I nod, my mouth forming into a straight line.

"Oh, I must tell you about this thing that happened at work today ..."

Maybe Ollie is right, and it was a stupid thing to do. Flirting or trying to flirt with a bunch of strangers ... anything could have happened.

My phone pings with an incoming message. I pull it out of my clutch and check it.

Sam: How's the night? Ready for me to call you and make an excuse?

Chloe: I already told you not to do that! Ignore her, Bel.

Sam: Why are you texting when you're in the other room, Chlo? *Rolling eyes emoji*

Chloe: Shut up!

Me: It's going ok. Ollie has been telling me about his job for fifteen years ... I mean minutes.

Sam: Argh, do men not realise we don't care about their jobs?

I let out a snigger.

"Everything ok?" Ollie asks, his eyes zoning in on my phone in my hands.

"Oh, yes, just the girls," I say, placing my phone back into my bag.

The waitress comes back over and places our wine glasses on the table. My eyes snap behind her, and my jaw drops open.

Entering the restaurant is Dominic, a beautiful woman standing closely next to him.

His eyes take in the surroundings and freeze when they land on mine. A surprised smile flickers across his face.

What is he doing here?

Come on, Isabella. It doesn't take a genius; he's on a date.

"Nico?" a high-pitched voice says, drawing my attention to his companion.

She's beautiful, wearing a light green satin suit. On anyone else, it would look ridiculous, but on her, it contrasts beautifully with her long, black, glossy waves.

"Nico, my boy!" An older gentleman rushes towards him and shakes his hand. "Lovely to see you again, and Nancy"—he turns his attention to the woman—"you're looking lovely as ever," he says, kissing her before standing back. "Your table is all set up for you, and we've got the champagne on ice."

"Mr. Romano," she says, smiling. "You do know how to spoil us."

"Please, this way." He blushes at Nancy as he leads the way.

Dominic's eyes flick towards us as he passes before taking a seat in the corner.

Far away from us.

Thankfully.

I pick up my wine and take a swig, my nose scrunching up at the taste.

"Are you ok?" Ollie asks, his eyes on my glass as he notices the size of the gulp.

"Excuse me, miss," a voice says, drawing my attention away. Standing next to our table is the gentleman who was speaking to Dominic, a tray in his hand with a single strawberry daiquiri on top. "Mr. Barone sent this over to you."

"Excuse me?"

"I said—"

"No, I heard you." The guy slams his mouth shut, confusion written across his face. I meet Dominic's stare from across the restaurant. "Can you thank him for me, but I will be paying for this myself."

He swallows and nods before turning around and heading back over to Dominic.

I feel the heat of Ollie's stare as I turn to face him. He arches his brow. "Friend of yours?"

"Friend is a strong word." I brush him off as I slide the strawberry daiquiri closer to me. I run my finger around the rim of the glass before sucking the sugar off. Dominic's eyes darken as mine clash with his.

Holy shit.

Am I playing with fire?

"Oh, right. He's not one of the men you were flirting with, was he?" Ollie barks out a laugh at his joke.

My mouth slams shut.

"I'll be right back," I say, not bothering to wait around as I rush down the corridor and rip open the bathroom door.

I take a deep, grounding breath.

How funny it is that we're both here at the same time.

Yet, he's with a supermodel, and I should come with a warning label: 'May cover you in strawberry daiquiri.'

Making my way towards the sink, I grab some cloth out of the holder and hold it under the cold tap before pressing it lightly against my neck.

I hate seeing judgment on somebody's face.

And Ollie had judged me, whether it was from a place of care or not.

Throwing the cloth into the bin, I catch my reflection in the mirror as I stand in front of it, my hands resting on my hips as I tilt my head to the side.

I've always had curves. It's something I used to struggle with growing up, but I'm a lot more comfortable with my body these days. My blonde, unruly, hair is a gift from my mother, and my blue eyes are the carbon copy of my father's. It's something I share with Jason.

I don't like comparing myself to anyone—we are all different in our own way—but the woman Dominic was with tonight ... she oozed elegance, commanding the attention of everyone in the room.

I could barely command my parents', let alone anyone else's.

The door opens, distracting my attention, and a lady enters. She shoots me a smile before heading into a cubicle.

I give myself one final look before I exhale a deep breath and pull open the door.

My steps freeze as I notice Dominic leaning against the wall opposite.

"Hi Shortcake," he says, a smile tugging at his lips.

"Hi," I say, the door shutting behind me.

"You look," he says, his eyes drifting over me, slowly, "beautiful." He takes a few steps closer.

"Thanks." I blush, my eyes dipping to my feet.

"Are you on a date?" he asks.

I shake my head.

"Does he know that?"

"Yes," I say firmly. "We're just friends."

His brow creases. "Friends don't look at you the way he does."

"How's that?"

"Like he wants to kiss you," he says, his eyes dropping to my lips.

My tongue darts out and wets them.

He reaches out, grips my chin, and tilts my face to his.

"Lose the date, Shortcake."

"It's not a date," I protest breathily, his spicy after-shave invading all my senses. "Anyway, you're one to talk."

His eyes harden. "I'm in a business meeting."

"Isn't this a little too fancy for a business meeting?"

He smiles. "Let me take you out on a date, and I'll show you the difference," he says, his thumb lightly brushing against my lower lip.

My eyes threaten to flutter closed, but I fight it.

"I'm ok." I swallow.

He smirks, his thumb pausing on my lips as he dips his head.

Is he going to kiss me?

My heart beats wildly against my chest as I brace myself for the first kiss I've had in a while.

The door opens behind me, and I fall back.

He catches me effortlessly, hauling me against his chest.

"Shit! I am so sorry!" A woman gasps behind me. "I didn't realise anyone was leaning against the door."

"It's fine," Dominic replies tightly as she rushes past.

I push my hands against his chest, but he doesn't budge.

I need to get away from him before we do something stupid.

"Dom, I need to get back to Ollie." I give him another light push.

He makes a low noise at the back of his throat, his arms releasing me.

"Join us," he says as I walk away.

I freeze and look over my shoulder. "You're joking, right?"

"Nope," he says. "Join. Us."

I shake my head. "No."

We have a silent battle as we stare at each other, nothing but the distant chatter of the restaurant behind us, as his eyes light up in amusement and he breaks the spell.

"I'll see you at the table, Isabella," he says, leaving me standing alone.

What the hell just happened?

Did I lose?

I give my head a subtle shake before pulling open the door.

Dominic stands, his back towards me, as he speaks to Ollie.

"I'm sorry, but I need to hear what Isabella says about this first," Ollie says, his eyes meeting mine, and he closes his mouth.

Dominic turns to face me.

"What's going on?" I direct my question to Ollie, ignoring Dominic's stare.

"This guy here—"

"Dominic."

"Right, Dominic," Ollie corrects himself. "Said we were joining them?"

I see the questions behind his eyes.

My head snaps to Dominic, and he smiles sweetly at me.

I sigh, turning to Ollie. "Is that ok?"

His shoulders drop. "You want to join them?"

I shrug.

I have a mini war going on inside my head.

The devil sitting on my left shoulder is screaming at me to be daring, maybe even a little unhinged. To eat dinner with Dominic and his date.

The angel sitting on my right wants me to leave Dominic alone. To realise we are from completely different worlds.

"Ok." Ollie sighs as he stands, grabs his drink, and reaches for mine, but Dominic beats him to it. Ollie's eyes narrow, his mouth forming a straight line.

We follow Dominic as he leads us to his table.

"Nancy, we have company," he says as he places my drink down and pulls out my chair.

Her head snaps up, and a frown covers her face. "Oh," she says, her eyes flickering between Ollie and me.

I clock a laptop and an iPad on the table.

Maybe this really was a work meeting.

I drop down into the chair as Dom rounds me and takes a seat opposite me.

"Hi, I'm Ollie." Ollie smiles sweetly as he takes the seat next to me, draping his arm over the back of my chair. "And this is Isabella."

Nancy's eyes flick to his arm, and I see her shoulders relax slightly.

"Nice to meet you both." She smiles, but it doesn't reach her eyes.

Dominic leans back in his chair, his legs outstretched, and his foot grazes mine.

God, someone get me another drink.

"So, Ollie, how do you know Isabella?" Dominic asks, a hint of something in his tone.

Irritation?

Dominic's eyes flick behind me, where Ollie's arm still rests on the back of my chair.

"How do I know Isabella?" Ollie repeats the question, his smile trained on mine. "I met her in art class."

Dominic's brow raises. "So, you both go to art class ... together?"

"Yeah," Ollie says, smiling. Dominic's eyes narrow a fraction. "We sat together, and well, what can I say ... the rest is history?" He points his question at me, and I feel the pressure.

I feel the heat rising in my cheeks as Dominic's hand pauses on his glass.

"You paint?" The question catches me off guard. I'm not used to people taking an interest.

"Yeah, mostly landscape. Have done since I was little," I say nervously, twisting the charms on my bracelet.

"What kind of landscapes?"

"Anything," I reply. "Whatever catches my eye in magazines, books. When I was growing up, we didn't have much money, so I would tear pages out of magazines in shops." I slam my mouth shut; I've never admitted that to anyone before.

"I used to steal chocolate bars," he says, and my eyes snap to his. A smile curves at his lips, and I instantly relax. "My mother was always strict about them; she said they would rot our teeth, so my brother and I would always steal one to share on the way home from school."

I smile. I can't imagine Dominic of all people needing to steal ... he looks too put together for that.

"So, do you have a goal in mind? Maybe your own art gallery?" he asks, and I'm instantly snapped back into reality.

My smile falls. "That would be the dream, but no. I paint for me right now, until I can pluck up any kind of courage to maybe organise a pop-up or something."

My own art gallery? Is this guy crazy?

His eyes search my face. "I think a pop-up is a great idea. Everyone has to start somewhere."

"I have the steak, medium rare?" the waitress says as people bring our food over to us, placing various plates on the table.

It takes a few minutes before it's suddenly overflowing with food.

Did Dominic and Nancy really order all this, just for themselves?

Nancy begins tucking in, grabbing some salmon, and adding it to her plate. "Nico, do you want some of this?" she offers, her hands pausing over the plate.

Dominic shakes his head.

I look down at my tomato soup and sigh, my stomach growling.

"Is that all you're having?" Nancy asks, her eyes snapping to my soup.

I nod, pulling it towards me before tucking in.

"Here is the extra champagne you ordered, Miss White," the waitress says as she places the bottle next to Nancy.

"Thanks!" She beams.

We all eat our food in silence.

I feel the weight of Dominic's stare as I look up, and I'm met with a frown.

What? I want to ask, but I keep my mouth closed.

"Please, help yourselves," he says, gesturing around the table. "We never eat it all, and Nancy seems to have overordered." He cuts his eyes to her, but she acts oblivious.

There's ordering, and then there's this.

"Thanks," I mumble, but I make no effort to touch anything else.

Ollie smiles as he leans across the table and heaps a load of potatoes onto his plate.

"Do you actually think you'll do this pop-up ... event?" Nancy asks from across the table.

"I ... I'll think about it," I reply.

"I know a few people—" Dominic starts, as he loads a plate with food, but I shake my head.

"It's fine, I have a few ideas, and hopefully—" The words die in my mouth as he pushes my soup to the side and sets the plate in front of me.

My mouth drops open as he gives me an encouraging smile.

"What are—"

"Eat."

I want to say no, to say that I don't accept charity ... but all this food, the chicken, the fries, the potatoes, the steak ... it screams at me, and who am I to deny it?

Picking up my fork with a grin, I tuck straight in.

"Thank you both for a lovely evening." I give Dominic and Nancy a smile as I reach for my bag on the floor. "Can we get the bill, please?"

"It's already taken care of," Dominic says, and my mouth snaps shut.

When the hell did he sort that?

"You're going to have to send me your bank details, Dominic," Ollie says next to me as he places his hand on mine.

Dominic's eyes narrow.

"I'd like to pay for Isabella's and mine. It's my treat tonight."

"Like I said, Ollie. I've sorted it." Dominic shoots him a dismissive look before turning his attention to me again. "So, when shall I mark off the date in my diary?"

"What date?"

"Bella—" Ollie tries to cut in, but Dominic shoots him a look and Ollie shrinks back.

"The date for the exhibition?"

I smile. "I'm a long way off yet."

"Make sure you tell me; I'd love to come."

"Bella, come on, I've only paid for three hours in the car park," Ollie says, reaching for my hand and pulling me to my feet, before stomping towards the door.

Dominic's jaw tightens, and for a moment I want to run my fingertips across it.

Fuck, I think the strawberry daiquiris have hit me more than I realised.

"Good night, Shortcake," he says in a low, husky voice. He brushes my hair off my shoulder and presses a kiss on my cheek.

"Thank you for the food," I mutter, turning to follow Ollie.

Chapter 8

Isabella

Ollie: Do you want me to pick you up?

Me: No, it's fine. I'm nearly there anyway.

Ollie: Ok. Save my seat.

My steps falter as I push open the door to art class, and my mouth drops open.

Dominic.

My eyes land on his broad back, the white shirt straining as it wraps around him. Feeling the weight of my stare, he turns around, his lips curving into a smile as they land on mine.

My mouth goes instantly dry at the sight of him.

His shirt is rolled up at the sleeves, revealing his thick forearms. His hair looks effortlessly styled, his stubble freshly trimmed.

He looks far too good for an art class.

"Shortcake," Dominic says as he makes his way towards me, pressing a lingering kiss on my cheek. The heat from his palm rushes through me as it rests on the bottom of my back.

Fuck, Isabella. Move, speak. Do something!

He steps back, his eyes dancing around my face, as I finally find my voice.

"Dom ... what are you doing here?"

I shrug off my jacket as I walk towards the corner, placing it on the hook next to Dominic's navy blazer. *They need to open a window in here.*

"The thing is, Isabella ..." he says as he stands a little too close. "I got the urge to learn how to paint the other night, and I thought, what better way to learn than an art class?"

Why does he always smell so damn good?

"You ... you want to learn how to paint?" I stumble over my words.

"Yup." He answers instantly. "And this class popped up first ... how coincidental."

"This class that is miles away from where you live?"

"How do you know where I live, Shortcake?" He arches his eyebrow, and my mouth instantly snaps shut.

A laugh rips through him, low and throaty.

I feel it to my core.

"Anyway, I thought this class was full," I tease.

He lowers his voice. "Funny, they seemed to be able to fit me right in." His cool, minty breath fans across my face with every word.

God, he's like a drug.

"Right, we're about to begin, so if you can all take your seats," Frankie shouts from the front, and it's like an ice-cold bucket of water has been thrown over me as I jump back.

Dominic smirks.

Rushing past, I take my seat.

"Great, an empty chair," Dominic says as he drops down next to me.

My eyes flick behind him. "I don't think it is empty ..."

His brows pinch together.

"Excuse me," Candy says to Dominic. "You're sitting in my chair."

He looks confused. "You have allocated seats?"

"Yup ... so if you could ..." She jerks her head to the side as Dominic's eyes flick to mine, and I shrug, sending him a smile as he lets out a breath and vacates her seat, only to find one a few spaces down.

A chuckle slips past my lips as he sits next to Ronnie, a lady in her sixties, who is looking for husband number five.

"Hi," she says bashfully as soon as he takes his chair.

"Hello," he says as he shoots me a look. *Sorry, honey, you're on your own there*, I want to say, but I settle for giving him a thumbs-up.

"Right, my lovies. Today is all about shading and line work," Frankie begins, and I turn my focus to her.

"Now if we could all pick up our B-pencils," she says as she grabs hers and presses it lightly against her canvas, "and begin shading. Start lightly. Don't press too hard. If you break the pencil, then you clearly have pressed too hard," she teases, looking straight at Dom, and we chuckle. "Now today, as you can see, we have a new face, so I will be floating more than normal."

"Excuse me, Frankie?" Dominic says, gaining her attention. "Which one is the B-pencil?"

"This one, sweetie," she says, picking it up and handing it to him.

He looks so cute, completely out of his element.

"Sorry I'm late," Ollie says as he enters the room. His brows tug together as he spots Dominic before he takes his seat on my other side. "Hey, Bella," he says, pressing a kiss to my cheek before grabbing his pencil.

"Ollie." Frankie gives him a nod before pressing the button on her computer.

Drum and bass blares through the speakers.

Dominic's eyebrows shoot into his hairline as a laugh rips through me.

I chuckle as I watch Dominic trying to shade—and failing. His gradients are about as smooth as my flirting.

"What's up?" Ollie asks as he follows my eyeline.

"Nothing, just watching Dom," I say in amusement.

Once Dominic reaches for a 4B pencil, I decide I can't take any more. I jump up and dart towards him, wrestling it out of his hands.

"Dom, 4B is used for darker shading. You know, to give a richer tone," I say, and his brows pinch.

I reach for his B pencil and show him my technique, tilting the pencil at an angle and stroking it against the page.

I gasp as I feel Dominic's hand grip my hips, and he tugs me down next to him on his chair, his body pressed against mine.

"Please, continue," he mutters, his face a feather stroke from mine.

My breath catches in my throat.

"Shortcake, you were helping me," he says quietly, his eyes focused on my lips as my tongue darts out and wets them.

Oh, yes. Shading.

Reaching up, he brushes a curl off my forehead, tucking it behind my ear.

"Ollie, is everything ok?" Frankie asks, and my head snaps in his direction, breaking the spell.

"Yes," he says, his glare focused on Dominic. "I just realised I have a doctor's appointment," he bites out before grabbing his things and leaving.

The rest of the class passes in a blur.

As much as I get lost in my work, I'm conscious of Dominic's presence throughout. Every time I steal a glance, he's already watching me.

"Shortcake," he says as I place my arms through the holes in my jacket. "Care to join me for a drink?"

"Not tonight," I say as I bend to pick up my bag, throwing it onto my shoulder. "I have a date." I finally turn to face him as a shadow passes over his face.

"Who with?"

"With Mr. Darcy," I say, trying to hide my smile.

It takes a moment for it to click. "Oh, you mean *Pride and Prejudice?*"

I shake my head, not bothering to hide my disgust. "Ew, no ... *Bridget Jones.*"

"Never watched it," he replies.

"You've never watched *Bridget Jones*?" I squeak, not bothering to hide my shock.

He shrugs. "Nope."

"You don't know what you're missing out on."

"Maybe we can watch it together sometime?" he asks, and I slam my mouth shut.

Maybe we could? It's only a film ... and technically I'll be educating him, because he clearly needs it.

"Maybe," I say shyly.

My eyes flick across his face. He seems relaxed. He has smudges on his face from the pencil lead, and his hair is sticking up in places from running his hands through it in frustration on many an occasion.

I think he assumed Frankie would be easy on him, but she wasn't. She didn't want him to sit there and not earn his place.

"How about a drink first?" he asks. "Then our second date can be a movie night?"

Second date? This guy is confident.

"Dominic!" Frankie waves, gaining our attention as she rushes towards us. "Well done tonight. I was pleasantly surprised. Your technique needs some attention, but it was a good job Isabella was on hand to help."

"Wasn't it just," he says with a smirk.

Frankie smiles at me sweetly as she pats his arm. "Well, I will see you next week. Good night."

He nods; his eyes fixed on me.

"Come have a drink with me," he says as he takes a step closer, and I feel the heat radiating off him.

"I ... I can't."

"Why not?" he asks, tucking his hands in his pockets.

"I just can't," I say before turning on my heel and walking away. "Good night, Dom."

I can't have a drink with someone like Dominic. Yes, he is beautiful to look at, and the odd flirt never killed anybody, but I just know this man would break my heart, and I don't think I could handle it.

So I'm protecting it with everything I have.

Chapter 9

Dominic

Isabella: I hope you've been practising for your next class.

Me: I have, but I think I need some extra tutoring.

Isabella: I'm sure Frankie would love to help.

Me: Don't make me pout.

"What time do you call this?" Joey asks as he falls into step with me as we make our way through our building.

"It's called eight am," I reply dryly as we jump into the lift.

"I got a call this morning ... from Nina," Joey says as he presses the button and the lift begins moving. "Seems Tony left confidential paperwork on his table at breakfast."

My hand tightens around my phone. "He did what?"

"Yup," Joey says, shrugging. "So, how are we going to play this? Good cop, bad cop?"

The doors ping open as we step out onto our floor.

People nod at us as we pass.

"Leave it to me."

All the chatter from the boardroom comes to an abrupt stop as we enter. The only noise is from the door clicking shut behind me.

"Good morning, everyone," I say as I make my way towards the window, pausing for a beat.

With our building located in Canary Wharf, we enjoy a perfect view of the buildings situated along the Thames. Wherever you are in the office, the view is outstanding; it's something that drew me in when Joey and I chose it.

I turn to face everyone, twelve sets of eyes on me.

Joey pours us both a cup of coffee before taking his seat. His eyes have a mischievous twinkle as they focus on Tony.

I turn my attention to the rest of the room, my eyes slowly flickering over every single one. They sit nervously as they wait for me to speak. Finally, my eyes land on my target.

He smiles, but it doesn't reach his eyes. His hands are clasped tightly in front of him, resting on the table.

"Tony," I say.

Tony swallows.

"Mr. Barone," he says, shuffling in his seat.

"How was breakfast this morning?"

His eyes widen a fraction at my question, his throat bobbing up and down. "Fine. Great."

"What did you have?"

"You ... want to know what I had for breakfast?" he asks, confusion flickering across his face.

I nod.

"Eggs Benedict and a vanilla latte."

"Must have been pretty fucking good, Tony."

"What makes you say that?" He stutters slightly, uncertainty flickering across his face.

"Because you left confidential paperwork on the table."

He shakes his head vigorously.

"I wouldn't try lying to me, Tony," I say as I stare right at him. "It's my goddam job to know the whereabouts of every single person that works at my firm."

People whisper around the table.

His mouth opens and closes.

I raise my hand, silencing him.

People think the moment they leave the office; their job is done. It's not. Once you represent a company, you represent them in and out of work hours.

“Don’t try and insult me, Mr. Brown,” I say, turning my attention to every single person in the room. “This was a rookie mistake. Our clients trust us, and if they can't trust us, then what chance do they have?”

“Dominic—” Tony interjects.

“It's Mr. Barone to you.” I cut my eyes to him, slamming my hand on the table, making everyone jump. “From this point forward, you do not work for Lusso. I want you to pack up your shit and get the fuck out of my building.”

“No!” He jumps up, his chair falling onto the floor.

“Security will be here to escort you off the premises in sixty minutes.” I check my watch. “Make that fifty-eight. Tick tock, Tony.”

Tony's worried gaze flicks around the room, looking for some kind of support from his colleagues, but he gets nothing. “You can’t do this,” he says loudly, his hands shaking.

“I think you’ll find I can do what the fuck I please,” I say, picking up the mug of coffee that sits in front of Joey and taking a sip. “And I plan to inform every law firm in London of your carelessness.”

The door to the boardroom opens, and two security guards enter.

Tony swallows.

"Gentlemen." I nod towards them as they take a step into the room.

Tony's eyes widen as he glances at me one last time, before his shoulders drop in defeat and he stomps out of the room. Security follows him, and the door clicks closed.

Silence fills the room, again.

I let it hang for a few moments before I speak.

"I shouldn't need to tell the rest of you my expectations. Tony abused the trust of not just me, but his client, too. I won't accept laziness. I certainly won't accept sloppiness. If any of you think you're not up to the job, then please leave now." I gesture with my hand towards the door.

Not a single person makes an effort to move.

"Then get back to work. We'll have another meeting tomorrow to discuss Tony's workload." I dismiss them as their chairs scrape against the wooden floor, and they all dart out of the room.

"Shit, talk about a mood killer," Joey jokes next to me as he leans back in his chair and crosses his ankles on the table.

I frown as I take a seat.

"So, shall I start the interviews today or leave it until tomorrow?"

"Tomorrow."

"Right," he says, pushing off the table and rising to his feet. "I have to get going; I have a date."

"It's the middle of the day," I say, shaking my head.

It could be the middle of the fucking night, and Joey wouldn't care.

He's a serial womaniser, and I don't blame him. He struggles to let people in, and he keeps his circle small.

"You know me, brother." He winks as he passes. "Oh, I meant to ask." He turns to face me. "What's this I heard from Nancy ... you're taking an art class?"

Fuck.

Chapter 10

Dominic

Me: I hope you're having a good day.

Isabella: I'm at work ...

Me: When you're not at work, what do you like doing?

Isabella: Paint, binge-watch series, anything that involves food. What about you?

Me: Work.

Isabella: Is that it?

Me: Yes, my work takes up a lot of my time.

Isabella: You need to get out, Dom. Live a little.

Me: I plan to.

"I thought we were coming to you," I say over my shoulder as I enter my office and notice Giovanni sitting on my sofa. I pour myself a coffee as I make my way over to him.

"I thought I'd save you a trip."

"How considerate," I say dryly.

"Nico, we have to ..." Nancy's words die in her mouth as she enters my office, her eyes widening as she spots me and Giovanni sitting on the sofa. "Hello, Mr. De Luca. I didn't realise our meeting this afternoon had been rescheduled."

He doesn't respond.

"Take a seat, Nancy." She does, her back straight as she focuses on Giovanni.

"Tell me why you want to work for me," Giovanni drawls lazily as he takes out his knife from his blazer and twists the blade over his fingers. "Do you think you are capable of filling Nico's shoes?"

"I know you already think this meeting is pointless. You don't want anyone but Nico working for you ... and if I'm being honest, it's wasting my time too, which, as you know, is precious."

Giovanni arches his eyebrow.

"I am an impeccable lawyer. I go above and beyond for my clients—something I have learnt from Nico, but also something I have perfected myself. You won't find another person like me, and something tells me you already know that." A smile tugs at her lips before she brushes it away. "Now, if you'll excuse me, I have a meeting. If you do find yourself considering me, just know that I work twice as hard as Nico." She gives him a nod before she rises to her feet and leaves, not sparing me another glance.

Silence fills the air. The meeting lasted no more than three minutes.

She worked that just as I thought she would.

Ruthless, cold, and intentional.

I flick my gaze to Giovanni, who stares at the door, a small smile on his lips.

He's pleased.

"Explain something to me, Nico," Giovanni says, clearing his throat, his mask of boredom firmly back in place. "What's your end goal here? Do you plan on leaving this life?"

"No." I shake my head as I straighten the sleeve on my blazer.

"Because you know there is no 'getting out.' You're in it now, and that's it."

His eyes search my face.

“I don’t plan on 'getting out,' but I have other commitments and not just you. I have a business to run. You can't just keep calling me and expecting me to drop everything else.”

“I can, and I do,” he bites back.

I let out a frustrated breath. “What do you say about Nancy?”

“Hmm,” he says, his eyes briefly looking out my window before they flick back to mine. “Give her ten percent of your cases.”

I nod. That’s a start.

“Before I go, I need you to get hold of that brother of yours. He’s gone AWOL again, and I have a job for him.”

I frown. “What kind of job?”

“Please, you know we don’t speak business where people are watching.” He motions towards the camera in the corner of the room. “I'll be in touch.”

Not long after he leaves, my door bursts open and Nancy strolls in.

Her hands are on her hips as she stands in front of me. "What did he say?"

I smile, but it doesn't reach my eyes. "I thought you had a meeting."

"I don't know what you're talking about." She smirks as she tucks a stray piece of hair behind her ear.

"Giovanni is too clever to be played. Remember that."

Her smile falls. "I didn't try to play him. I simply said what we were all thinking. It was pointless. He's never going to hire me, and do you know what?" She crosses her arms as she shoots me a look. "I couldn't give two shits anymore."

I pinch the bridge of my nose.

Dropping down on the sofa in front of me, she lets out a frustrated breath. "The money is good, but it's not just that. I would have done it for you." Her face morphs into a frown. "You need a break from him. I see exactly what he does to you."

"Nancy." I shake my head. "I don't need nor want to speak about this."

"Nico, that guy is toxic ... actually, he's worse than toxic. He's the devil, and the longer you're around him, the more I see a change in you. God, we should have cut him off, like your father said to, years ago."

"You know it's not as easy as that." I pause. "And if you'd let me speak, you would have found out that

Giovanni has given you a small percentage of clients." A smile covers her face. "Welcome to the madhouse. I hope you don't regret it."

She tugs her bottom lip between her teeth for a few seconds. "About damn time."

"I think from this point forward, we need to keep things professional," I say.

Her face changes quickly, her brows pinching together. "Professional?"

"Yes."

"Why?"

"We always knew what this was. A little convenient fun."

She pauses. "It wasn't just fun to me," she says softly. "Is there someone else? That girl ... Isabella?"

Her question catches me off guard.

I knew she wasn't stupid. I knew the moment I brought Bella over to our table that Nancy would clock my intentions. The intentions I laid on a silver fucking platter that Isabella seemed oblivious to.

"I saw the way you were looking at her." I hear the hurt in her voice. "I just want the truth. For once in your life, Nico."

"There isn't anything to tell, Nancy," I say, rolling my tense shoulders. I may be a dick at times, but I don't like hurting her. We grew up together, experienced a lot together ... and whether or not she likes to admit it, we're like family. "Yes, she intrigues me, and I want to see where it goes, but she may not even want to do that herself."

"She will," Nancy says, tears glistening in her eyes before she blinks them away, her cold mask slipping back over her face. "I saw the way she was looking at you, too. I need to go. I have a meeting across town." She stands and strides out of my office.

Pulling my phone out of my pocket, I find Isabella's number. My finger hovers over the screen before I press the message button to text her.

Me: How about that date?

Fuck. I loosen the collar on my shirt as I wait for a reply. Dots immediately appear on the bottom of the screen before disappearing again.

My phone vibrates in my hand with an incoming message.

Isabella: What date?

A laugh slips free.

Me: I thought you didn't like games. *Winking emoji* I'll pick you up tomorrow.

Isabella: It always depends on the game, Mr. Suave.

Isabella: Tomorrow's fine. Nothing fancy, though, please.

Me: Leave it with me.

Nothing fancy?

"Sandra!" I say, loudly. My door opens, and my PA pokes her head around the door.

"Yes, Mr. Barone?"

"A date ... nothing fancy. What do I do?"

A smile touches her lips. "Maybe the movies? A walk in the park?"

Bingo.

Chapter 11

Dominic - Age 8

"Listen, Matteo, we fucked up!" my father yells from down the corridor.

They've been holed away in my father's office since they came home.

It sounds like a glass smashes against his door, and I jump back.

"I fucking told you! And look where it's got us!" My father's voice wavers.

"Boys," Rachel says as she walks towards me, gripping my upper arm and dragging me away from my father's office. My feet catch on the red carpet runner. "You shouldn't be here. Giovanni ... does your uncle know where you are?"

Giovanni shakes his head, his black hair falling over his eyes as he brushes it back.

My mother has taken Alessandro out for the day with Grace, our nanny, but I hadn't wanted to go ... so I'd stayed with Rachel, the housekeeper. She was young, fun, but she wasn't Grace. She didn't know what she was doing when she looked after us, so we got away with a lot. When I knew it was safe, I snuck Giovanni in through the back so we could play in the garden.

"Nico, I have to go home now." Her eyes soften as she looks down at me. "I can't bring you both home with me, and I don't know what to do." She chews on her nail as she looks behind me towards my father's door, where the yells get louder.

"My father's home," I say quietly, and her eyes flick to mine. "He'll look after us."

"We'll be ok," Giovanni mutters next to me as he bumps his shoulder with mine, forcing me to smile. "Go."

Her eyes drift to my father's office door for a few seconds before she cups my face. "Make sure you don't go into that room, Nico."

I nod.

Pressing a kiss to the top of my head, she grabs her bag and darts down the corridor.

"We need to pack everything we can and get out of here," my father says tensely, gaining my attention as I press my ear back against his door.

"Come on, Nico," Giovanni says. "We should go."

I wave him off.

"No, we can stay here, Tomasso," my uncle, Matteo, protests. "I can sort this."

"Sort this how?"

I hear someone banging against the front door loudly, and I stand up straight.

A loud bang shoots through the air, and there's a short scream—Rachel's scream—before a thud.

Was that gunfire?

My father's door is ripped open, and I notice a gun in his hand, before his wild eyes land on mine.

"Nico ... what are you ..." His words die in his mouth as he spots Giovanni behind me, his brows pinching together. "Gio?"

"Hi, Mr. Barone," Giovanni says behind me as the noise gets louder.

"Fuck!" my father growls as Matteo appears next to him. "Get Giovanni. We need to hide them in my office." He scoops me up in his arms, Matteo following with Gio. Slamming the office door behind them, they carry us behind his desk and towards his cabinets.

I can't hear anything over my pounding heart.

After opening the cabinet, my father pushes everything to the side and shoves me inside, and Giovanni climbs in after me.

"Whatever you hear or see, no matter what happens, you close your eyes and don't come out of this cabinet," he rushes out, pulling boxes in front to hide us. "This is to cover you, so they don't see you."

The noises get closer and louder.

My father's panicked face is the last thing I see before he shuts the cabinet and flicks the lock.

"What is the meaning of all of this?" my father says as he rushes out into the corridor and shuts his office door behind him.

I try to calm my breathing down, scared they'll hear me.

"Well, well, well," a deep voice says. "Who's been naughty, then?"

My heart practically stops beating.

"Do you know who I am?"

"Yes." My father's voice sounds so small compared to his. "Roberto De Luca."

My eyes snap towards Giovanni, who tenses next to me.

His uncle?

A deep laugh rips through the corridor as I push the boxes further in front of me, pressing myself tighter against the wall. "Bingo! Now, where is my nephew?"

Silence fills the corridor as my heart pounds in my ears.

"He's not here."

"I don't believe you," Roberto snaps. "Giovanni ... come out, come out, wherever you are."

Gio goes to move the box out of the way, but I stop him. Nothing good will come from his uncle seeing him here.

His head whips in my direction, and I press my finger against my lips.

"Check every room, make sure there's no one here, and if you see that little shit ... you know what to do," Roberto says, before my father's office door opens, and he comes strolling in. "Nice office you have here. You must be making some money."

"I do alright," my father replies hesitantly.

"Alright?" Roberto scoffs. "You've been selling on my turf. Taking my money. And now you dare insult me?"

My father's mouth slams shut. Sweat drips down his face as he stands rigid and Roberto strides up to him, stopping once they're toe to toe.

"You need to think before you speak around me, Mr. Barone," Roberto says, his jaw tightening as he takes out his gun and points it at my father's chest.

My tears drip down my cheeks as my heart pounds even harder.

"I apologise, Mr. De Luca," my father says calmly, his eyes focused on Roberto's face and not the gun he has pointed at his chest. "I didn't mean to speak out of turn."

"Well, you did. And for that, there will be consequences. Your wife is a very pretty thing, isn't she?"

My father's jaw tightens, but he remains silent.

"It would be a shame if that pretty face of hers got wrecked."

My father jolts forward, but Roberto's gun clicks, the safety catch off, and he halts, his chest rising and falling.

"Don't be stupid, Barone." Roberto tuts, a sinister smirk on his face.

"Mr. De Luca," Three armed men enter my father's office. "We've checked everywhere. There's no one here."

Roberto curses as he spins around, picks up my father's bottle of whiskey, and throws it across the room. Shards of glass land everywhere, and I jump.

"Keep your eyes peeled, and if anyone returns, tell me straight away."

"Yes, Sir," they say before leaving us alone.

"Mr. De Luca, perhaps we can come to some sort of arrangement," Matteo says. "You see, we didn't know this was your turf."

"You know, all I hear are a bunch of words," Roberto says sarcastically, as he strides towards my father's desk and takes a seat, resting his feet on the dark wooden table. "And I hate hearing people babble a bunch of shit. Now, let's talk business. Who's your supplier?"

"A family member."

"I didn't ask for a family fucking tree. I want a fucking name."

"His name is Dante Barone. He lives in Italy, and he sends us shipments every month," my father says.

"When's the next one?"

"Tomorrow."

He taps his gun against my father's desk, a smile on his lip.

"You'll inform my men of the details. From this point forward, you work for me."

My uncle takes a step forward but pauses when Roberto points the gun at him.

"You want to take a shit? You inform me. You want to buy a new fucking tie? You inform me."

"Roberto—" Matteo begins, but Roberto cuts him off.

"If you keep speaking over me, I will have to show you how low my patience is."

My father's hands shake as his jaw tightens. He shoots Matteo a glare, and Matteo slams his mouth shut.

"Good little doggy."

Everything happens so quickly.

Matteo reaches inside his pocket and pulls out his gun, pointing it at Roberto.

But Roberto is faster.

My eyes squeeze shut as my uncle's screams ring in my ears.

Chapter 12

Isabella

Chloe: Where is he taking you?

Me: I have no idea.

Sam: You have no idea? He could be a serial killer.

Chloe: I think that's a little extreme, don't you?

Me: Just a little?

Chloe: What are you wearing? *Eyes emoji*

Me: I don't think it matters what I'm wearing.

Sam: You're right. It matters what you're wearing underneath. Tell me you're wearing cute underwear?

Me: *Tumbleweed GIF*

Chloe: Oh, for crying out loud, Isabella!

"You really thought this out, didn't you?" I smile as I look down at the picnic blanket laid out on the grass.

Dominic has driven us to a park in Sevenoaks, Kent, and it's beautiful. There's greenery for miles and oak trees lining the paths that run through the field. People go about their day. The only noise is from a distant barking of the dogs that are out with their owners on a stroll, or a few children playing football, or kicking the crisp autumn leaves in the air.

"I wanted to take you for a meal," Dom says, gripping the back of his neck, looking down at the basket. "But I know you said you didn't want anything fancy ... so I thought of this."

I smile.

This is miles better.

"But if you'd prefer, I know of a cute Italian down the road?"

I shake my head. "Dom, this is perfect."

His eyes snap to mine and hold. "Are you sure?"

"Yes."

He shrugs off his blazer and takes a seat on the red chequered blanket, stretching out his long legs.

A comfortable silence fills the air as I look out onto the park. The orange leaves on the trees sway in the wind, and I want nothing more than to pick up a paintbrush and capture this moment.

"Penny for your thoughts?" he asks, gaining my attention.

"I was just thinking how I would love to paint this."

Dom's ringtone blares, and he checks the caller ID before declining it.

"I don't think Frankie would say I'm ready yet." A soft chuckle slips through his lips and washes over me. "But," he says as he reaches inside the blanket and pulls out two tiny canvases. "I thought we could maybe have our own private art class?"

My breath hitches.

He continues to pull things out of his Mary Poppins basket as he lays out all the supplies on the blanket.

"Dom ... you really brought all of this here?"

Paintbrushes, paint, a water bottle, a jug, and a packet of pencils.

"I wanted it to be special." His eyes darken as they drop to my lips for a moment.

"Painting is one of my favourite things. I always dreamed as a little girl that I would have my art in galleries ..." My voice trails off as I chuckle at the thought. It's unlikely to happen at this point. "But it was never meant to be." A sudden sadness washes over me as I pick up a pencil and start shading the corner of my blank canvas.

"Never say never," he says as he squeezes my hand, and my eyes snap to his. "Maybe one day, you can show me your work?"

"Maybe," I say. I clear my throat. "So, welcome to Isabella's art class. This will be different from any other class you will ever attend."

"How so?" Dominic says, smiling.

"Because I will tell you how terrible you actually are at art," I say, a laugh ripping through me, and Dominic's eyes widen in shock before he chuckles.

"I hope you do, gives me time to perfect my technique," he says in a low, husky voice, and my thighs immediately clench together.

Reaching forward, he tugs me towards him as I add the colours to the palette, my hands tremble at the proximity.

"So, I was watching you in class, and you hold the brush completely wrong," I say, clasping his hand in mine and placing the brush between his fingers. "We always start by lightly placing the brush into the paint. Don't dunk like a biscuit into a cup of tea." I feel him smile next to me as he remains silent. "We only dab, getting a tiny amount of paint on the tip." I have the smallest amount of paint on the tip of my brush before I lightly stroke it across the canvas.

Dominic scoots closer to me as his body presses next to mine. I feel his breath fanning across my hair as he leans up, brushing it over my shoulder. Goose bumps dance along my skin.

"Are you concentrating?" I ask breathlessly.

"One hundred percent," he mutters as his lips brush against my neck with every word.

"Dom, what are you doing?" Our hands pause on the canvas, mine tightening around his as my eyes threaten to flutter closed.

"I think you know what I'm doing," he says, reaching for my chin. He turns my head to face him as his eyes flick down to my lips. "I'm going to kiss you now," he says before closing the distance.

The moment his lips brush mine, a wave of electricity rushes through me. I want to deepen the kiss, but I know it's not the right time.

We are in the middle of the park, in public, and I'm trying not to have a heart attack.

His tongue pushes against my lips as I open up to him, and the moment his tongue strokes mine, I melt into him as he takes control.

A soft yip breaks us from the earth-shattering moment, and we push apart.

"What the fuck?" Dom says, his brows pinching together.

A little French bulldog yips again, butting his head against my hand.

"Hey, little guy, where's your owner?" I coo, as he continues to rub his head on my hand.

"He looks like he needs a bath." Dominic's eyes sweep over the puppy, who stumbles over his feet. He's not wrong— a thick layer of mud covers his light brown fur, and leaves are stuck to his paws.

Where are your owners?

The little guy seems to have taken a liking to me, as he drifts off to sleep curled on my lap.

"I'll go see if I can see someone," Dominic says, jumping up and walking away.

"Why are you alone, hey, buddy?" I whisper, stroking his head.

You're talking like he's going to answer you back. I laugh at the thought.

"Shortcake," Dominic says as he stands above me, "there's no one else around." He scratches the back of his head.

"I'm not leaving him here." I'll sit here all night if I have to.

"What do you want to do?"

I look down at him, my eyes softening. A warmth hits my chest.

I always wanted a dog growing up, but we could barely feed ourselves, let alone anything else.

"Can we take him to the vet?"

Dominic's head tilts to the side, his eyes searching my face. "Let me just pack everything up."

"Wait," I say, making him freeze. "Let's eat first. Then we can go."

"Are you sure?" he asks, and I nod.

He takes a seat, reaching into the basket.

"I'm sorry the date isn't going as planned."

"Shortcake, I wouldn't change it for anything," he responds as he passes me my sandwich before ripping open his own.

The puppy's eyes snap open as he stumbles to a seating position.

"I don't think so, buddy." I tap him on the end of the nose.

"Buddy?"

I shrug. "Just until we find his owners."

Dominic's head tilts to the side as he tries to read me.

Good luck, pal.

Ripping open his sandwich, he begins tucking into it as I sit watching him. His Adam's apple bobs up and down as he swallows. He looks out of place here, sitting in his expensive suit, but he seems relaxed, and I like it.

"If you keep looking at me like that, Shortcake, I'll have to continue what we started earlier."

My mouth slams shut. I want nothing more than for him to kiss me right now.

"I'll Google the nearest vet," he says with a soft chuckle.

Disappointment washes over me.

"Thanks," I say quietly as I finish my sandwich. Buddy climbs off my lap and stumbles over to Dominic, a low growl emanating from him.

"What?" Dominic says to Buddy.

"I think he wants your sandwich," I say, chuckling softly.

"Really?" he says, raising his eyebrow before letting out a frustrated breath and holding it out to him.

"Dom," I rush out, and Dominic yanks his hand back. "He can't eat half a sandwich! He'll choke!"

He rolls his eyes but tears a small piece off and holds it out to Buddy, who takes it gladly.

"Look at you two ... bonding."

"I wouldn't call it that." He scoffs.

I hesitate for a beat. "Can I ask you a question?" He nods. "So, you and Nancy?" The moment the words leave my lips, I regret them. I tear the remaining sandwich into pieces as I hear him sigh.

"What do you want to know?"

"Is she an ex-girlfriend?" I continue to look down at the sandwich in my hand, as Buddy nibbles the bread from his.

"No," he says. "We grew up together, we were good friends, and I guess somewhere along the way, the lines got blurred."

"So it was never anything serious?"

"Never. Or at least, not on my part, although I was always clear it would only ever be purely physical. I put a stop to it the moment I met you."

“Mr. and Mrs. Barone?” the vet calls, carrying Buddy under his arm.

“Oh, I’m not his wife.” I chuckle awkwardly.

Dominic remains silent.

“I apologise,” he mutters before clearing his throat and placing Buddy onto the table in the middle of the room. The moment his paws touch the cold metal table, he rushes towards me, bumping me with his head.

“The little guy here isn’t microchipped.” His eyes soften. You read about it all the time: dogs being left to fend for themselves; dog homes overrun because they can't rehome them. “Now, I’m not sure what you plan on doing here. We can keep him here and hope that we can find him a new home in time... or you can take him?”

A sadness washes over me. As much as I would love nothing more, we aren’t allowed pets in our flat. It’s the one rule Phoebe and Manny won’t negotiate on.

“I’m sorry; I can't.” My voice cracks.

The dog gives me sad eyes.

Don't do that. I would take you if I could.

"I'll take him," Dominic offers, his eyes focused on me.

"Really?" I ask, not hiding the surprise in my tone.

"Yeah," he says, clearing his throat, a crease appearing on his forehead.

I launch myself at him, wrapping my arms tightly around his waist. "You're amazing."

His phone rings again, and he declines the call again, a frown appearing on his face. "Come on," he says tightly as he picks up the puppy. "I need to drop you home."

Chapter 13

Isabella - Age 13

All I've wanted all day is to get home and paint. Paint whatever came to mind.

At least now, I have something to keep me company at home, especially since Jason has been gone so much.

After running all the way home, I push open my front door and dart straight to my bedroom. Kicking off my shoes, I throw my old rucksack onto the bed before reaching beneath it.

Empty.

What the hell?

"You won't find your art things, Isabella." My mother's voice trails off as I sit up on my knees. She rests against the doorframe, checking her chipped nails.

"What do you mean?" I rise to my feet, my voice coming out choked, as I try to hold back the tears.

She sighs as she pushes off the doorframe and closes the distance between us. Her hand brushes my tight curls off my face. "We needed the money."

"What?"

"I sold it," she says so calmly.

My breath leaves me in a whoosh. How could she?

"Sold ... sold, it?" I stumble over my words as she smiles at me, but it doesn't reach her eyes.

Does she not feel guilty?

"Come on, you're not stupid. It's a waste of your time. Just an expensive hobby. I've done you a favour, really. I mean, getting your hopes up like that? Who does that teacher think she is? People like us don't *paint*."

Chapter 14

Dominic

Joey: You're late.

Joey: Are you ignoring me?

Joey: Seriously, are you dead?

Joey: I get your Bugatti.

"What?" I snap at Buddy; the dog Isabella instantly fell in love with.

Am I jealous of him? Yes, I am.

After the vet cleaned him up, he told us he was roughly one year old. Practically a baby.

Where are his owners? How could anyone abandon something so small?

I've never wanted a dog. I don't have the time or patience, but seeing Isabella's eyes staring at me when she told them she couldn't take him ... it made something snap inside me.

Buddy lets out a low bark, trying to gain my attention.

"I'm trying to work here," I say, gesturing to my computer.

Today is the first time in a long time that I've worked from home. I thought it was best not to leave Buddy alone on his first day here.

There's a knock at the door. "Who's here, Buddy?"

Fuck, I think I've gone mad.

I pull open my door, and my smile drops. "I think I need to have a word with Charles about who he allows up onto my floor."

Charles is the head of security of the building, and he is damn good at his job ... or so I thought.

I turn on my heel and make my way back to the table.

"I wanted to see if you were dying," Joey says as he closes the front door and follows me in. "Because that's the only explanation I could think of for you working from home for the first time in ... well, ever."

A low growl sounds behind me as Buddy sits at my feet.

Joey's eyes snap down to him.

"Since when have you owned a fucking dog?"

"Since yesterday," I roll my shoulders. "He's a stray."

A smirk appears on Joey's face as he leans down and holds out his hand. Buddy walks hesitantly towards him, sniffing his hand, before his whole bum shakes in excitement. Joey scratches behind his ear.

"If you have something to say, then fucking say it, because I have a call with a client in a minute."

"It's just ..." Joey chuckles to himself. "Dominic Barone owning a dog. I never thought I'd see the day. Then beautiful Isabella comes along, and all of a sudden ..."

A growl leaves my lips involuntarily.

"We were on our date, and this little guy crashed it." Buddy rushes back to my side, sitting at my feet. I frown at him but lean down, stroking behind his ear.

"He seems to like you."

"No, he just knows I'm the one who feeds him."

The doorbell rings.

"Expecting company?" Joey arches his eyebrow as he turns and opens the door. "Well, well, well, what do we have here then?"

"Erm, hi," a small soft voice says. Jumping up, I rush towards the door and push Joey out of the way. "I'm Isabella."

"Isabella, hey," I say as my eyes drift down to the bags in her hands. I lean forward, taking them off her. "Come on, I'll put the kettle on."

"Thanks," she mumbles quietly, her cheeks reddening.

"There you are, Buddy." She drops to her knees as Buddy rushes excitedly towards her, and she instantly peppers him with fuss.

"Jealous of a dog, dude?" Joey whispers before barking out a laugh.

"Fuck off," I say out of the corner of my mouth, so only he can hear.

Isabella stands in front of us, Buddy safely tucked under her arm. "I'm sorry to turn up without calling." She blushes slightly. "Charles downstairs is a right peach. Did you know he knows Manny? He let me straight up, no question. I hope that's ok."

I remain silent. I put her on the list the moment I got back after our date.

"Still going to have a word with Charles?" Joey whispers to me, and I elbow him in the stomach. "Fucker," he says, coughing.

Thankfully, Isabella is too engrossed in fussing over Buddy to notice.

"But you did give me your address and told me to turn up at any time." She lets out a nervous laugh as she continues. "I thought it was only fair for me to bring some things, considering I think the only reason you agreed to keep Buddy was because of me."

She stops right in front of me, the top of her head reaching my chin. I smile down at her as she passes Buddy into my arms, and I scrunch my face up as he stares right into my soul.

Keep looking at me like that, and I'll quit feeding you.

"So, I've got him a lead," Isabella says as she turns on her heel and pulls out the contents of the bag, laying everything on my kitchen island. "I've got him a few choices of food, because we don't know his favourite yet."

I feel the weight of Joey's stare.

"I also got him—well, and you—a little gift." She blushes as she reaches inside the bag, her hands wrapping around something, and she pulls it out, a huge smile appearing on her face.

Joey's laugh echoes around my apartment as Isabella holds out a white dog bowl with "my daddy loves me" printed across the front.

"Isn't that cute?"

I cut my eyes to him.

"Sorry," he mumbles, trying to regain control.

"It's ok. I'll get you an 'uncle loves me' bowl too for when you babysit?" Isabella arches her eyebrow at him, and Joey's mouth slams shut.

She's a firecracker, this one, and I fucking like it.

"Yes, Uncle Joey," I say, a smirk on my face. "Buddy can't wait for you to look after him."

Joey shakes his head. "I'm good, thanks."

"Shame," Isabella mutters as she folds the bag up and places it in her handbag, taking a seat on a stool. Her face rests on her palm as her eyes dance between us.

"So, Jojo, are you staying for a cup of tea? It would be nice to get to know you."

"Actually, I am." Joey smiles sweetly at her as he pulls out a stool.

"Don't you have work to do, *Jojo*?" I say, narrowing my eyes at him.

"Nope, I'm fine here," he says, ignoring me.

"Stop being a killjoy, Dom." Isabella rolls her eyes at me, and my mouth drops open.

Killjoy?

Placing Buddy onto his feet, I pour us all a cup of tea before resting against the counter. My eyes drift between Isabella and Joey.

"So, do you work with Dominic?" Isabella asks.

"Work?" Joey arches his eyebrow at me. "Dominic never works ... I mean, look at him. He's practically pulled a sicky today."

"Joey," I warn, and he smirks. "I haven't ever pulled a sicky, and I never plan to, either."

"What do you do, Isabella?" Joey asks after sipping his tea. "Nico, pass me a biscuit."

Rolling my eyes, I pull a packet out of the cabinet and throw them at him.

"I'm a waitress," she says nervously, fiddling with her charm bracelet. "But I'm working on my art. Who knows, maybe one day you'll see my work in a magazine or something." A nervous chuckle slips past her lips.

"Is that what you want?" Joey asks, and she nods. "Well, Nico knows a lot of people—"

I shake my head, and he changes tack.

"Bella, we need to meet up sometime without this old grump." He hooks his finger in my direction. "There are some stories I can tell you about him."

"Really?" Her eyes light up in excitement.

"Yeah." He smiles as he carries his mug to the sink. "Right, I need to head back. The office will fall apart without me." I scoff. "Nice seeing you, Isabella."

"Nice to meet you," Isabella says back as he closes the door behind him.

Silence fills the air; the only noise is from Buddy lapping at his water.

"Why did you agree to have him, Dom?" Her question catches me off guard.

I tip her chin up, her eyes meeting mine. "I hated seeing you sad; it tugged at something inside of me. You're too beautiful not to smile."

Her eyes drop to my lips, and her throat bobs up and down.

I lower my voice as my thumb strokes her bottom lip. "Spend the day with me."

"The day?" she asks, her breath fanning across my lips. "I think you're asking too much, Dominic."

I smile.

"Oh, baby, I live for pushing the boundaries. You haven't seen anything yet."

She laughs, a warm, rich sound. Her eyes drop to my lips once more.

My phone rings, cutting through the thick tension as I drop my forehead against hers.

"Fuck," I whisper, and she chuckles.

"Go answer that; it's probably important."

"Will you stay?"

She nods.

I press a kiss against her forehead and grab my phone off the counter. "Mr. Southwell, thank you for getting back to me ..."

Chapter 15

Isabella

Chloe: What do you mean he left you to have a meeting?

Sam: Tell me you're snooping?

Me: No! I am not going snooping … that's rude.

Sam: No, it's not! At least you can make sure he isn't a serial killer.

Me: And how am I going to do that exactly? I don't think he would keep dead bodies here. *Rolling eyes emoji*

Sam: You never know. Some of the shit I've watched, they hide them in their car.

Chloe: It's true. People are crazy these days.

I think he'd been about to kiss me again. And what's crazy is that I want him to. Since the park, I haven't been able to stop thinking about anything else.

The way his lips felt against mine, the way he brushed my hair off my shoulder ...

I wait a few minutes as I pace his kitchen before deciding to take Sam's advice and have a little look around.

The kitchen is a chef's dream ... it's clean, huge, and seems as if it's never been used. The light from the pendants hanging above the kitchen island makes the glitter in the marble worktops sparkle. My hand runs across the sleek tops.

Floor-to-ceiling glass panels reveal a terrace that seems to wrap around the whole place, overlooking Knightsbridge. All the lights from the streets below would be an amazing backdrop.

The only view I have from my window is the alleyway behind Wilson's. I'm lucky if I don't look out and find a drunk guy urinating against the bins. I grimace at the image.

Dom's light beige sofas sit in the middle of the open space, and I compare them to the mismatched sofas back home. His huge flat-screen TV is fixed above a stone fireplace, and I can't help but tamp down my excitement at the prospect of watching Damon Salvatore on that.

Making my way down the corridor, I push open the doors and sneak a glance into each room. They're all decorated the same: cold, clinical, white. No character.

Where are the paintings? The scatter cushions?

I push open the last door on the right and make my way inside.

This must be his room.

A dark oak bed sits to my right, with black sheets.

Two black sofas sit to my left, facing the TV on the wall. Dark brown laminate runs throughout.

This has more character, even if it is very bachelor-pad.

I push open another door to reveal a walk-in closet. Most women's dream.

My dream is a huge open space, where I can paint and not be disturbed.

Closing the closet door behind me, I open the oak door next to it, revealing a huge, family-sized bathroom. My mouth drops open at the size of the bathtub, my hand trailing over it. I can't remember the last time I had a bath.

The black marble tiles reach from floor to ceiling. A huge mirror stretches across the vanity unit, where there are two sinks.

Did someone live with him ... before?

"Shortcake." I spin around to face him. He looks amused, leaning against the doorframe.

"Shit." I clear my throat and try to come across more confident than I feel, considering he's just caught me snooping. "I was just looking for the bathroom ..."

A smile tugs at his lips. "All the way back here?"

"Yup," I say, popping the P.

"I don't mind you snooping, Shortcake," he says, pushing off the doorframe and striding towards me. "I have nothing to hide."

He stops right in front of me and brushes the hair off my face. "Did you find anything interesting?"

"Nope," I mutter as his hand strokes my face. "You're a pretty boring person."

A laugh rips through him. "You know, I really like you, Shortcake. I haven't been able to stop thinking about that kiss," he says quietly as he closes the distance between us, stopping when his nose brushes mine. "Have you thought about it?"

The earth-shattering kiss?

"No," I say breathlessly.

"Maybe you need reminding."

His thumb continues to stroke my cheek as he kisses me softly. His soft lips mould against mine as the electricity runs through us. The heat from his hands presses tightly against my sides, seeping through the material of my clothes. His tongue brushes against the seam of my lips, and I open up for him, and the moment his tongue strokes mine, my heart skips a beat.

He tears his lips from mine, pressing them against my forehead as he whispers, “Come on, let's walk Buddy. He’s waiting for us.”

Chapter 16

Isabella

Dominic: When can I see you again?

Me: You only saw me the other day.

Dominic: Buddy misses you.

Me: Of course, and I miss Buddy.

Dominic: Just Buddy?

"How are you feeling?"

"Oh, you know me, sweetie," Phoebe says, patting my cheek. "I'm a soldier; it's going to take more than a broken bone to get me down."

Phoebe was a pain in the ass. Even when she broke her foot, we couldn't keep her away from this place. She perched a chair behind the counter, and that was it.

"I told you to take it easy," I say, my eyes softening. "You need to lean on us girls."

I motion my head towards Chloe, Sam, and Georgina.

"I know, sweetie." She smiles sweetly. "But this place is my baby, and being away from it ... I don't know what to do with myself. Anyway, enough about me." She waves a hand. "We want to hear all about your date with that delicious guy."

"How do you know he's delicious?" I say.

"Samantha told me."

Sam shrugs.

"Well, he picked me up and drove me to Kent," I say. Phoebe's eyes widen. "It was beautiful. We went for a little picnic, and we saw deer, and then we picked up a stray dog."

"A ... dog?" Phoebe asks, shocked.

"Yup. He's called Buddy, and he now lives with Dominic."

I struggle to hide the smile that appears on my face.

Chloe smiles sweetly at me.

"What?"

"Nothing," she says, "It's just nice to see you dating again."

"It was one date; I'm not planning on marrying him."

Georgina snorts next to me, and my eyes snap to her. "Sorry, I didn't mean for that to come out."

"What?"

She sighs, throwing the rag she's holding onto the counter. "All I'm saying is be careful."

"Be careful?" My brows pinch together. "Do you know something I don't?"

She shakes her head, her eyes widening. "God, no! I just mean men, in general, can be tricky."

Why do I feel like she's keeping something from me?

"I think what Gee here is trying to say," Phoebe interjects, patting Georgia's hand, "is that no man can be trusted until he proves us otherwise?"

I hum. Is that what she's trying to say?

"Anyway," Chloe says, changing the subject. "I think we need to plan another night out, and this time Georgina is coming with us."

Georgina's eyes cut to Chloe. "I don't think that's a good idea."

"Why not?"

"Because I've never been out before." I hear the nervousness in her voice.

"You'll be fine with us," I say, reassuring her.

"Maybe," she mutters quietly, her hands winding together as she tugs her bottom lip between her teeth. "Can't we have a night in instead?"

I shrug. "That's fine with us!"

“Good.” Georgina lets out a relieved breath. “Can it be at yours? It's just I’m having work done at mine, so we won't get any peace.”

“Ladies,” Ollie says, gaining our attention from the entrance. “Bella, how are you? Ready for our dinner date?”

“Hey Ollie, I’m good, although I don’t finish for another hour ...” I feel everyone's eyes on me.

“Can’t you wrap up early today?”

His question lingers awkwardly.

“It's fine, Bel,” Phoebe cuts in. “Go, we’re quiet anyway.”

“Are you sure?”

“Perfectly sure.” She smiles sweetly at me, but it fades slightly when she looks at Ollie. “Go, enjoy, and I'll speak to you tomorrow.”

I blow her a kiss as I round the counter.

“I’ll be right back!” I call over my shoulder as I disappear out the back.

I jog upstairs, grabbing some black shorts and a matching T-shirt, shove on my black trainers, and throw my work uniform into the laundry basket as I pass.

I lock up behind myself and find Ollie leaning against his car out front.

His eyes drift down my body before he opens the door. “You know, with you on shift work, we can't hang out as much as I’d like,” he says in a clipped tone.

"I have to work, Ollie," I respond flatly as I climb into the car.

He rounds the bonnet and jumps in, pulling into the busy streets, chaotic with Ubers and buses at this time of day.

His words linger in the air.

The idea of being stuck at home, all day alone, brings up memories from my childhood. Memories I do not welcome. I never want to feel *alone* again, and that's why a house share with my girls is the best thing to happen to me.

Pressing my head against the window, I watch the streets pass us by as Ollie heads further out of London.

Mariah Carey's "Obsessed" is playing quietly in the background as I drum my fingers against the door.

"Here we are," he says, drawing me out of my day-dream.

Chapter 17

Isabella

"Fuck." Ollie slaps his hands against the steering wheel, his car coming to a jerking stop on the way home after sharing a pizza.

"What's wrong?" I ask.

"I'm going to go check," he says, his eyes drifting over my face before he jumps out, opening the bonnet.

I follow. "Do you know what it could be?"

"Yeah, it's scrap," he says, shaking his head and slamming the bonnet shut. I jolt back. "It's been on its way out for a while now, but I thought I had more time." He turns to face me. "I'll call for a recovery. Sorry, Bel."

"Hey." I reach out and rub his arm, his eyes dropping down to it. "It's not your fault; things happen."

He smiles tightly before turning on his heel and making the call. I'm just glad I don't own a car, because there's no way I could afford to maintain it.

After a few minutes, he comes back, a defeated look on his face.

"It sounds like we're going to be stuck here for a couple of hours."

My mouth slams shut. Hours?

"But, luckily for us, I just so happen to have a blanket and a bottle," he says, smiling as he rounds the car and opens the boot. After a few seconds, he comes back, laying the blanket out in front of us and taking a seat. I follow.

He opens the bottle of vodka, takes a sip, then passes it to me.

"So, tell me something no one knows about you, Bella."

"Something no one knows?" I say, scratching my chin. "I've been collecting random things from places I visit since I was a kid."

His brows pinch. Was he expecting me to go deeper? *Sorry, pal. I'm not ready.*

"Like what?"

"Like ... if I go into a restaurant, maybe something with the logo on. Or a nice pepper shaker."

Ollie scrunches up his nose as I continue.

"Maybe a nice stone from a park."

"A stone?" He scoffs, and my mouth snaps shut into a thin line.

Judged—that's how I feel whenever I'm around Ollie.

I take a sip before passing it back to him.

"What about you then?" I say as I wrap my arms around myself. "Tell me something about you that no one knows?"

He takes a huge sip from the bottle. "I've only ever been with one girl," he says, a crease appearing on his forehead. "They don't tend to go for guys like me."

"I'm sure that's not true," I say softly.

He rolls his eyes as he passes the bottle back to me.

"Don't be silly, Isabella." He scoffs. "Girls like men who are wrong for them. I bet you've been hurt in your past." He pauses for my reply, but I simply nod. "See?"

Ouch.

I clear my throat, suddenly not wanting to speak anymore. "Ollie, I don't want to talk about my previous relationships."

"I'm sorry," he rushes out, his hand grasping mine. "It's just that the good-looking men aren't always the right ones."

I remain silent. I'm ready for this night to be over.

My phone pings with a message as I pull it out of my bag, needing the distraction.

"You answer that, and I'll grab us another blanket," Ollie says, jumping up and leaving me.

I unlock my phone and see I have a message from Dominic.

Dominic: I've found myself at a loose end. What are you doing tonight? Do you want to come over, and I'll order us food?

Me: I can't. I was out for pizza with Ollie, and his car broke down; we're waiting for recovery.

The bubbles appear and disappear a few times on the screen before his message pops up.

Dominic: Where?

Me: I'll speak to you later. Kiss Buddy from me

Dominic: You can kiss him yourself when I come and get you. Send me your location.

I do exactly that as Ollie drops back down next to me, draping the new blanket over our legs.

"Everything ok?" Ollie asks, his eyebrow raised as he looks at my phone.

"All good," I reply, placing my phone back in my pocket.

"Can I ask you a question?"

"Of course." I turn to face him, passing him back the bottle.

"Why won't you date me?"

My mouth opens and closes a few times.

An awkward silence fills the space.

I sigh. "I only see you as a friend, Ollie."

"I know," he bites out. "But explain to me why."

I let out a breath. "I'm sorry if that's not what you want to hear, but it's true, and it will never change."

A shadow crosses his face. "You've never even given us a try."

His eyes drop down to my lips, and a smile covers his face.

"Ollie, I think you've had too much to drink."

"No. I've never thought more clearly," he rushes out, edging closer.

"Ollie, no," I say, scrambling to my feet to put some distance between us.

"Come on, Bel." He presses again, this time reaching for my arm and tugging me closer. "I think we could be pretty fucking good together."

"You barely know me," I say quietly, tugging my arm away.

His brows pinch as his eyes clash with mine.

My breath catches as he jolts forward, his lips nearly brushing mine, but I turn my head quickly and they graze my cheek instead.

"Never do that again," I snap, even though my heart is beating a hundred miles an hour.

"I'm sorry," he says, a wave of panic crossing his face as he tries to reach for me again, but this time I'm faster. I take a huge step back and cross my arms over my body, creating a barrier.

"I am so sorry, Bella," he says, holding his hands up in surrender before tucking them into his jeans pockets.

"Shortcake?" I hear Dominic's voice as he strides towards us, his eyes narrowing on Ollie.

Thank God.

A wave of relief rushes through me.

Dominic reaches out and tugs me towards him, his arms wrapping around me.

"Are you ok?" His eyes search mine, and I nod.

"Dominic, how are you?" Ollie says, clearing his throat. "I didn't realise you were coming. I can get Isabella home."

"It's fine. I'm here now," Dominic says tightly, his tone less friendly. "Grab your things."

I nod my head as I rush to the car and grab my jacket.

"We can't leave Ollie," I whisper.

Dominic's eyes narrow for a second before he nods.

"Ollie, jump in," he barks as he opens the passenger door for me.

The black leather seats mould perfectly to me as I snuggle into them.

Dominic smiles at me before shutting the door.

Dominic's knuckles are turning white as he grips the steering wheel. The rich scent of leather fills my senses as the plush black chair envelopes me. A smile touches my lips at the navy-blue stitching. It matches his suits. The huge digital dashboard lights up as he sets my chair to maximum heat so I can get comfortable. I feel like I'm sitting on a cloud.

"Thanks for picking us up, Dominic." Ollie says. "I would have gotten Isabella home safely."

Dominic doesn't answer him; his eyes focused ahead on the road.

Ollie trails off his address, and we sit in silence, Dominic's hands still wrapped tightly around the steering wheel.

Once we pull up, he barely makes it out before Dominic peels away from the curb.

"What's wrong?" I ask.

The heat from the heaters is too unbearable. Reaching forward, I turn it off.

"Nothing."

"Liar," I bite out.

His eyes cut to mine. "I don't want to talk about it right now."

"Pull over," I say, and his face changes. The frown he was sporting disappears. "I said. Pull. Over."

He sighs before acquiescing.

I waste no time in pulling open the door and climbing out. "Thank you for the lift. I can see myself home from here," I say before slamming the door and storming into the darkness.

I pick up my pace, walking further into the dark alley. The stench from the local bins invades my nose, I have no idea where I am, but I know I'll find my way ... somehow.

I've had enough tonight with Ollie's snide remarks. I don't need Dominic's attitude too.

A car door slams, but don't bother turning around.

"Shortcake." I hear Dominic's voice behind me, but I keep on walking. His fast footsteps approach before he reaches for me and spins me around, backing me up against the cold, dark wall. The only light is from a dim streetlamp a few feet away. I can't read his face. "Don't ever walk away from me again," he says, fury behind his eyes.

"Then stop being an ass," I reply, my chest rising and falling.

“An ass?” I hear the humour in his voice, but I choose to ignore it.

Has he never been called that before? I highly doubt it.

“Yes, you were trying to kill your steering wheel with your hands. Your jaw was ticking like crazy.”

His lips curve into a smile, his hand reaching out and tilting my head up, and he looks into my eyes, the shadows half covering his face.

“You're driving me fucking crazy,” he whispers, his breathing heavy.

“You're driving me crazy,” I repeat, my heart beating rapidly.

“Fuck it,” he says in a low, gruff tone.

He leans closer to me, his lips slamming against mine, his body pushing me against the wall as I moan into the kiss.

The moment his tongue touches mine, it sparks something inside of me, something I’ve never felt before. Raw, primal passion. I want to give myself completely to him.

His knee pushes my legs apart, and he presses it between my thighs, the friction making me gasp as I buck my hips against him. He continues his movements as I ride his thigh in this dark, dingy alley. Between the fierceness of his kiss, the pure passion of it, and the pressure building from his leg rubbing against me, I’m so close I could cry.

"Take it, baby. Use me," he whispers against my lips, as he brushes his hands between us, drifting beneath my shorts. The moment he touches my wetness, he growls into my mouth.

"Fuck, Shortcake." He groans. "Is this for me?"

I nod against his chest. Not being able to form any words.

"All of this," his hand strokes me lightly, tormenting me, "is it for me?"

"Yes," I say breathlessly.

"Come for me, baby." He pushes his fingers inside of me, easing them in and out slowly, in a steady rhythm. "I want you to squeeze my fingers." My core rushes to his demands as I clench around his fingers. A low growl slips past his lips.

I shake my head against his chest, my heart rate beating out of my chest.

I'm so close.

He continues at a steady pace, his mouth moulded against mine.

And I come undone from someone else's hands for the first time in a dark, dirty alley.

Chapter 18

Isabella

Jason,

It's been 2555 days, and with each one, it gets easier knowing I will have you home soon.

I think I have met someone. He's nothing like Myles... Maybe this could turn into something? I can't wait for you to give me your approval – if that's ever possible, lol.

Anyway, I need to hurry. Today is my favourite day, because I get to see you.

I love you, Bro. <3

I place the note with the others in my box and tuck it under my bed as the taxi outside honks.

Locking up behind me, I rush down the path and climb into the Uber.

"Hello ma'am," the driver says, smiling as he peels away from the curb.

"Hello," I mumble back. Resting my head against the window, I stare out, looking at the streets as they pass by in a blur. Since Jason got convicted, I make sure to visit him when I can. Ten whole years without him, and it doesn't get any easier. I promised him I would live for the both of us, and once he was released, we could experience everything he had missed out on ... and so far, I've experienced nothing.

"Who are you visiting today?" His question made me frown until I remember I had to put in my drop-off location.

"My brother," I reply quickly, my eyes flicking back to the window as I let out a breath.

"My cousin, Ricardo, is in prison," he says, shaking his head, his hands gripping the steering wheel a little tighter. "He's done some bad things. Very, very, bad. He killed someone."

My mouth slams shut as I mask my shock. *Why is he telling me this?*

"They say prison changes a person ... it can be for the better ... or worse." His words linger in the air for a few minutes.

He's right in that respect.

"Your brother ... will it be for the better?"

His question catches me off guard.

"I hope so."

The Uber comes to a stop outside the prison.

"Thank you," I say quietly as I climb out.

"Miss," he says, halting me from shutting the door. "Good luck to your brother."

"Squirt?" Jason's voice makes me snap my head up. All the emotions I feel every time I see him come rushing to the surface as I jump up and wrap my arms around him. "Crying again? Anyone would think you haven't seen me for months," he jokes, but it falls flat.

My brother rarely shows emotions, and since being locked up, he has gotten worse.

Prison has changed him; he's a lot harder now. Before, he used to let people walk all over him, taking his fair share of beatings. But now, after seven years of spending most of his time working out, people are frightened of him. Being six foot four and full of muscle, I can see why he intimidates most people.

But to me, he's always been a teddy bear.

"Sorry, sorry." I wipe my tears as I take a seat. "I can't help it."

I rub my arms, trying to warm up from the cold chill in the air. This room is always freezing. It doesn't matter what time of year it is.

"I know you can't, squirt." I see the love he has for me every time he smiles. "Not long and I'll be outta here."

I nod, no words forming.

I love seeing my brother smile; it isn't something he does much of anymore.

"So, how are Phoebe and Manny? They looking after you?" he asks as he grabs his coffee, pulling it towards him.

"They are."

"That's good." His eyes flick around the room, taking in every detail. The chipped pale blue paint on the walls, the plastic chairs we sit on, the metal table separating us. "What about you? How's your art? Did you start that class?"

I swallow. "I did. It's going well."

He smiles. "That's good. You need to send me some pictures, so I can see."

I nod, making a mental note to do so.

"I'm thinking about finally organising that pop-up."

His eyes light up. "That's a great idea. You need to live your life, not wait around for me. You've wanted to have your art in galleries all your life ... so, strive for it and you'll succeed."

I nod, letting his words sink in.

Maybe I should give this a go? What's the worst that can happen?

He takes a sip of his coffee. "What else is new in your life?"

Here goes nothing.

I never lie to my brother, and I don't plan on starting now.

When everything happened with Myles, it killed him to be stuck inside, helpless. I always promised him that if I met anybody else, he would be the first to know.

"Well." I clear my throat. "I've started seeing someone, I think ... well, I mean, can you call it 'seeing' if you've only gone on one date? I mean, he's taken in a dog because of me, which I don't know if he actually wanted to do or not."

"Isabella." He cuts across me, and I slam my mouth closed. "Chill a second." He lets out a breath before continuing. "Start from the beginning. Who are you seeing? You'd better not say it's that asshole again."

"Who?" I frown. "Myles?"

He nods.

I scoff. "His name is Dominic." I blush, and my brother notices. I can already see the distrust across his face. "He's a great guy. He's funny, generous ... well, he has to be, because of Buddy. I don't even think he likes dogs?" I say, tapping my finger against my chin.

Jason sighs. "I don't care about him; I care about you."

"I know."

"I want to meet him."

"I don't think that's a good idea ..."

"Why not?"

"Because ..." The words die in my mouth; I don't have a viable excuse.

"Exactly." A smirk tugs at Jason's lips. "Next visit, bring him."

"Jase ... why don't we see if it goes somewhere first? Then I'll bring him." My palms begin to sweat.

He raises his eyebrow. "I said. Bring. Him."

Fuck.

Chapter 19

Isabella - Age 17

"Thank you," I say over my shoulder as I leave the local art gallery, a new book in my hands. I'd managed to save up as much money as I could find to finally purchase it.

My phone rings, and as I pull it out of my bag, I notice it's an incoming call from a withheld number.

"Hello?"

"Bella?" I hear Jason's voice, but it's different.

My brows pinch together. Isn't he supposed to be at work?

"Jase?"

"Argh, fuck Bel ..." He sighs. "It's time."

The world stops.

People push past me as I stand in the middle of the pavement, but I pay no attention.

"Listen, Isabella, I have two minutes. You need to grab what you can and go."

My brother has always drilled into me time and time again that if the day ever came and he got caught doing things he shouldn't, I needed to grab everything he had hidden and dispose of it. It doesn't matter how, as long as it's nowhere near the house. He has hidden some cash too, somewhere our parents would never find it, and I'm the only other person who knows exactly where it is.

"Are you coming home?" My voice cracks.

"No," he replies. I know he is trying to hold it together for me, but I hear the emotion in his voice. "I fucked up, Bel. I'm going away for a long time. So, you need to go, make a new life for yourself ... exactly what we spoke about."

"But I don't want to. Maybe we could use the cash, get you a good lawyer?"

He lets out a frustrated breath, "Don't waste this money. Go to London, and when I'm out, I'll join you. I love you, squirt." And with that, he cuts the call.

I stand still for a few seconds, staring at a blank screen on my phone, before my brain finally kicks into gear and I take off running home.

I tear through the front door, my heart beating out of my chest. I sprinted all the way here, not stopping once, my mind focused on one thing.

My steps come to a halt as I spot my parents, my father half asleep in his chair, and my mother in the kitchen.

"Ah, there she is!" Mum slurs, stumbling towards me, wrapping her hand tightly around my bicep. "Did you hear what your brother has been up to?"

"We need to speak to a lawyer. It could have been a mistake. Maybe someone is setting him up?"

Her hand tightens on my arm, and I wince. "You really think we could afford a lawyer, Isabella?" she spits. "Look around." She motions behind me, and my eyes land on the threadbare sofas, the once-red carpet now covered in stains. "We can't even afford new furniture, and you expect us to find money for a lawyer?" She tuts as she looks at me in disgust. "Your brother has always been stupid. The moment I found out what he was up to, I tried to stop him. He's not clever enough to get away with it. But he didn't listen, and now look at him. He didn't think about us and the state he'd leave us in. He's fucking selfish!"

I rear back, her hand remaining on my arm, as I try to tug it free.

Selfish? I could laugh. This woman dares to spout that word at me? Does she not realise it's a parent's job to look after their children, and not the other way around?

"How can you speak about him, like that?"

"Like what?" She drops my arm and strides towards the fridge, pulling out a bottle of cheap white wine and flicking the lid onto the floor. "I'm just telling you the truth. You think he tells you the truth?" She pauses, and I remain silent, trying to control my rage. I've never wanted to hit anyone before, but the urge I'm feeling right now frightens me. "I do pity you sometimes, you know. Innocent little Isabella, always thinking the sun shines out of Jason's ass ..." She shakes her head as she takes a sip straight from the bottle. "You're going to have to start standing on your own two feet from now on. I won't support you anymore."

"When have you ever?" I bite back, and she grinds her jaw.

"You'll learn some respect." She slams the bottle down on the side as she stops right in front of me. "Otherwise, I'll teach you." My heart pounds in my chest. "Go to your room, Isabella, and when you come out tomorrow, you're going to get yourself a job and help pay the bills." She stops right in front of me. I smell the strong stench of alcohol pouring out of her. "Or you can pack your shit and be a disappointment to me, just like your brother."

I take off running to my room, grabbing the suitcases off the top of my wardrobe as I throw in clothes for myself and everything that I might need before pushing the door open to my brother's room. My mouth drops as I enter. His belongings are strewn everywhere. His drawers are open; the contents are in a pile on the floor. Ransacked. Thankfully, we knew they would do this, so we always made sure never to keep anything here.

We hid everything in the soffits in the loft. It's somewhere our parents never went.

Sitting on the edge of his bed, I wait until my parents crash out ... it won't be much longer.

How could Jason get caught? I drop my face in my hands as I rest on my knees.

He's always been extra careful ... making sure never to put himself in a situation that would end up like this. Then what happened?

After about half an hour, I sneak into the living room and spot my parents passed out on the sofas. Their mouths open as their chests rise and fall. An empty bottle of beer rests on my father's growing belly. Not wasting any more time in case they wake up, I dart out of the room and grab the duffel bag my brother hid in his wardrobe before I climb up into the loft, pushing everything out of the way until I find what I'm looking for.

A huge black rucksack full of jewellery.

Zipping it back up, I push my hand further into the mess until it wraps around a smaller bag.

Bingo!

I pull it out and shove it into my rucksack before grabbing everything I can and fleeing for London.

Where it's time to start again.

Alone.

Chapter 20

Dominic

"Nico, there's an Isabella here to see you?" Sandra says.

A smile tugs at my lips as I straighten my tie. "Let her in," I say, cutting the call.

After a few seconds, the door opens slowly, and a hesitant Isabella pokes her head around it. Once her eyes meet mine, a slow smile covers her face and she walks in, closing the door behind her. Her light blue dress enhances the shade of her eyes, and she's holding a brown paper bag in front of her like a suit of armour as she rocks back and forth on her white trainers.

"Hey." Her eyes flicker around my office. "Nice place you have here. Very fancy."

I remain silent as I watch her take it all in.

Her eyes finally land on mine again as she pauses in front of my desk. "Oh, I mean. You've probably got meetings ..."

She's right, I do.

"Take a seat." I motion towards the chair opposite me.

She lets out a breath before dropping into it.

"Can I get you anything? A cup of tea?"

She shakes her head.

I lean back in my chair, just staring at her.

She's the most beautiful woman I've ever seen.

I have to clasp my hands tight in my lap to stop myself from reaching across the table and pulling her into my lap. The need to kiss her perfect, red lips is almost too much.

"Actually, may I have that cup of tea please?" she rushes out, and I nod.

Rounding my desk, I head over to the cabinet in the corner and make us both a drink, bringing over the milk and sugar on a tray and placing it down in front of her.

I take my seat as I watch her rip open the sugar packets, some spilling onto my desk as she tips the rest into her cup, before adding milk.

I press the tips of my fingers against my lips, a smile threatening to spill.

If this were anyone else, their messiness would have annoyed me no end, but it amuses me how oblivious she is.

"One more," she mutters to herself as she tries her tea and pulls a face.

She rips open another sachet, and this one goes everywhere. Her eyes widen. "Oh, shit!"

"It's fine." I chuckle softly as I reach for one, tearing off the corner and tipping it into her cup, stirring it with my spoon before pushing it back towards her.

"So, Shortcake. To what do I owe the pleasure?"

"I was in the neighbourhood. Thought I'd come by, say hi." She holds up the paper bag and places it on the desk between us. "I bought you a sandwich."

I arch my eyebrow, as I slide it towards myself. "Thanks, Shortcake."

"How's Buddy?"

"He's fine," I lie. He's as chaotic as she is, constantly messing up my penthouse, leaving little messes for Grace and me to clean. "He misses you, though."

Her eyes snap to mine and hold; she bites her bottom lip between her teeth.

"Maybe I could come see him this weekend?"

"Buddy would love that," I say, smiling. I can't believe I'm using a dog as an excuse to see her. *Grow some fucking balls.* "Can I cook for us?"

She nods, her cheeks reddening slightly as she smiles down at her hands.

I've never cooked a meal for anyone before. I prefer to keep people out of my apartment, but with Isabella, I want her to see my life. To see that I'm more than a fancy suit and an expensive car.

The office phone rings. "Yes?"

"Nico, your one o'clock is here ..."

“Tell them I have to rearrange.” My eyes zone in on Isabella, who stares out the window.

“Ok ...” I hear the uncertainty in Sandra’s voice as I end the call.

She isn’t the only one shocked; I’ve never cancelled a meeting in my life.

“What would you like to eat tonight?”

“What can you make?” she says, smiling. “Because I don’t fancy food poisoning.” She pauses, waiting for my reaction.

“I’ll have you know, I’m a talented cook.”

Her eyes light up. “Really?”

I nod.

“Ok ... how about my favourite? A chicken tikka masala?” She shoots me a look, like she’s trying to challenge me.

Bring it on, baby. I live under pressure.

“Perfect,” I reply, adding that tidbit to my mental note of the things she likes.

“So, truthfully, what brings you here? I don’t think Canary Wharf is on your way home.”

Her fingers start playing with the charms on her bracelet.

“Isabella,” I say, and her eyes snap to mine.

“It doesn’t matter.” She tries to brush me off, but I don’t let her.

“It does.” I round my desk and sit in the chair next to her. “Tell me.”

"It's my brother," she begins. I tug her hand away from her dress and hold it in mine. Her eyes are focused on our hands, resting on my thigh. "He ... he wants to meet you."

"That's fine," I reply quickly. "Bring him tonight."

"It's not that simple," she mutters before tugging her hand away and standing up quickly. "It doesn't matter; I need to be going." She rushes towards my door.

"Wait," I say, her hand pausing mid-way to the door handle, but she doesn't turn around. "Why isn't it that simple?"

Her shoulders rise and fall as she lets out a breath. She turns to face me, and I see every emotion flicker across her face. "He can't come because he's in prison."

"Ok." That doesn't necessarily matter. I know more good people in prison than I should.

I motion with my head towards the sofa in the corner. She drags her feet to it before dropping down. I sit next to her as she lounges back, her eyes closed for a second.

"He did some fucked-up shit years ago," she says, her eyes still closed as her head leans on the back of the chair. "He's seven years into a ten-year sentence."

I remain silent, noting all this down in my head.

"He only did what he had to ... that doesn't make him a bad person." Her voice cracks at the end as her eyes meet mine.

I grasp her hand in mine. “It would be my pleasure to meet your brother, Shortcake.”

She gives me a tearful smile.

“I know he’s the most important person in your life ... and I hope one day I will be second.”

Her breath catches in her throat.

“Nico, I think we need to ...” Nancy’s voice trails off as she enters the room, an iPad held between perfectly manicured fingers.

Does she not know how to knock?

“What is it, Nancy?” I try to hide my annoyance.

“I didn’t realise you had company,” she says.

“Is it important?”

“It can wait a moment,” she says as she begins pulling the door closed, but pauses. “But only a moment. It's pretty urgent.”

“I’ll get going,” Isabella says, looking at me as she begins to stand, but I stop her.

“It's fine. Stay.”

Isabella frowns, her eyes flicking towards Nancy, who remains rooted on the spot.

I arch my eyebrow at Nancy, and she shakes her head before she takes a seat opposite us.

“I didn’t know who else to turn to,” Nancy begins, her eyes fixed firmly on me. “But I received a nasty note the other day, slipped under my front door. I thought nothing of it at the time—you know how people can be in our line of work. Until today ... there was a second one." I clock the worry across her face as her hands trail the edges of the iPad.

"What kind of note?"

"Oh, Nico," she rushes out, tears glistening in her eyes, but she blinks them away. "Here." She holds out a crumpled piece of paper

I take it from her, opening it.

Another skirt? You really like being watched, don't you?

My hands tense on the note as Isabella leans over my shoulder, reading it. She gasps.

"When did you receive this?" I ask, my eyes tracing the letters. "And why didn't you inform me immediately?"

Nancy tenses. "I'm sorry."

The anger inside of me is bubbling to the surface as I tamp it down. Isabella doesn't need to see that.

"I'll call Kingston. Get him straight onto this."

Isabella leans across the table, passing Nancy a tissue.

Nancy gives her a watery smile as she takes it, dabbing under her eyes.

"Nancy," Isabella says softly. "Dominic is cooking for me this weekend. Would you like to join us?" My stomach drops. I was hoping it would just be the two of us.

Nancy's eyes flick to mine.

"I don't think that's a good idea," Nancy mutters quietly, her eyes dropping down to the tissue in her hands as she begins playing with it.

"Please," Isabella pushes her. "I think it would do you good to get out of your head for a few hours. I mean, I can't promise good company ..." She flicks her head towards me and chuckles.

A small smile tugs at Nancy's lips. "I'll think about it."

Chapter 21

Dominic - Age 11

"So, what do you want to be when you grow up?" I say as I swing upwards again, my legs going higher than Gio's.

"I don't have a choice." His smile drops, replaced with a frown.

"Why not?"

"Because my uncle Roberto says I have to go into the family business." He shrugs as he looks out over the park. From here, we can see the whole of it. The trees are scattered around, the green leaves rustling in the wind. A group of kids plays football, arguing over who scored a goal. I've never been into football, no matter how much my father tried.

Kids are jostling to get down a green slide, its paint chipped. Alessandro pushes them all out of the way.

"Can't you just tell him you're not interested?" I ask, rolling my eyes.

He scoffs. We stop swinging and kick our feet on the gravel, the dust flicking high in the air as he wrecks his black trainers. "You know my uncle; he doesn't know what the word 'no' is."

"Giovanni!" a familiar voice barks. My stomach drops. "What have I told you about playing with these ... children?"

Roberto reaches for Giovanni and tugs him off the swing, his disapproving glare fixed on mine.

I glare back.

"We were just playing, Uncle," Giovanni rushes out as he's yanked behind his uncle, his feet dragging along the floor.

"Well, enough," Roberto snaps as he stops and bends so he's eye level with Giovanni. "If I see you with these lowlifes again, it'll be the last time you step outside."

Giovanni nods, his shoulders dropping.

Roberto rips open the car door and shoves Giovanni in the back seat.

"Roberto," my father shouts as he slams his car foot and darts towards us. "I think we need to calm down," he says, his breath coming out heavy.

Roberto cuts his eyes to him as he takes a step closer to my father. "Do you really think you're in any position to tell me what to do? Don't forget you work for me."

"Roberto—"

"No," he growls as he pushes his jacket back, revealing his gun.

A shadow of panic crosses my dad's face before he moves out of the way, grabbing me and shoving me behind him.

Roberto scoffs before jumping in his car and peeling away, leaving black marks on the tarmac.

"Fuck," my father exhales. Alessandro comes running over. "I don't want you two anywhere near that boy anymore."

"But papa—" Alessandro tries to protest, but our father raises his hand, cutting him off.

"No buts. My word is final."

Chapter 22

Dominic

Joey: You cancelled your meeting. Where are you?

Me: Quit checking up on me, and concentrate on your own calendar.

Joey: Someone's touchy. When was the last time you got laid?

Me: Fuck off.

Joey: Sounds like that's what you need … I can set you up, if you'd like.

Me: No.

The door opens, and my head snaps up from my phone.

A prison officer comes in, Jason following.

He's a lot bigger than I expected, his clothes straining against his muscles.

In the file I'd managed to pull up, Jason's picture was of a skinny kid, but the man in front of me is completely different.

Prison changes a person.

Jason glares as he sizes me up. He doesn't have trust in people, and I respect him for that. In this world, there aren't many people you can rely on. "Who are you and what do you want?" he grits out, standing with the cuffs biting into his hands. "I don't need a new lawyer; I already have one."

"A shit one at that," I say, raising my eyebrow.

"He's done me alright."

"Yes, he's done fine." I clasp my hands in front of myself. "So fine that you could try your hand at early release, but he never mentioned it."

Jason's eyes cut to mine and narrow. He doesn't believe me.

"Look, no offence, mate, but from the look of you, I couldn't afford you," he says, his eyes drifting over me and his lip curling in disgust.

I'm used to people seeing my expensive suit, the car, the watch, and immediately thinking I'm an arrogant bastard. They wouldn't be far wrong. But I'm also a ruthless bastard. I will stop at nothing until I get my client what they deserve.

And Jason is about to become my client.

"So let's save ourselves from wasting any more time here." He turns his attention to the prison officer. "Amberson, take me back to my cell. I'm done here."

Amberson nods, tugging the cuffs towards the door.

"Wait," I say, and Jason pauses. "I'm here because of Isabella."

At the mention of his sister's name, he turns to face me. His brows pinch together. "Look, I'm sorry she sent you. But we—she—can't afford it."

"I don't want her money."

Jason observes me for a few seconds. "It's you, isn't it?"

"Me?"

His jaw tics. "You're the guy. The guy she's started seeing."

A smile threatens to tug at my lips, warmth spreading through my chest—but I bat it down, for now, to focus on the most important thing in her life: her brother.

"Yes, I'm the guy she's dating," I confirm, straightening the cuffs on my shirt. "Now, please sit. Let's talk about that early release."

I gesture to the chair opposite me.

"What are we doing, Bennett? Are you staying or not, because I'm missing *Four in a Bed.*"

Jason's eyes snap to mine. "I think he's come a long way, don't you? Perhaps I'll hear him out."

Amberson nods as Jason holds his hands out and Amberson uncuffs him, before standing by the door. "You're lucky it's on record," he mumbles quietly.

"Quit moaning," Jason says before he takes a seat opposite me.

Amberson rolls his eyes.

"How did you meet my sister?" he asks as he watches me.

"We met at a nightclub in Soho," I respond, leaning back in my chair. "Your sister is quite something."

A laugh rips through Jason.

"That she is." He pauses. "I don't even know your name."

"Dominic. Dominic Barone."

"Well, Dominic. Isabella has had her heart broken before." My brows pinch as he continues. "I don't want to get her hopes up about this when there's no certainty of it." He motions to all the paperwork in front of us. "I think it's best if you just leave her—us—alone."

An awkward silence fills the air.

"You know I'm not going to do that, don't you?" I say. He goes to speak, but I cut him off. I lean forward in my chair, levelling him with a look. "I'm one ruthless, calculated motherfucker, and I will stop at nothing to make sure that the people I care about are happy."

He cocks his head to the side. "If you think you know Isabella so well, tell me something about her."

"Well—"

He cuts me off. "Not the usual shit that you could find out on her social media. Something not many people know."

"Isabella likes to collect things. A coaster, a piece of tissue with a logo on, from places she has been." His lips curve into a small smile. "Most recently, that has been a dog from the park, which now, despite my better judgement, lives with me."

A chuckle slips past my lips, but I clear my throat to compose myself. "Whether or not you believe me, she makes me feel ... and that is not something I'm used to. She makes me feel ... alive again. Like I have something to live for other than work. I'm in this for the long haul, and I'm not going anywhere."

Jason remains motionless for a few minutes before he leans forward, holding out his hand to me.

"Then welcome to the family."

Chapter 23

Isabella

Ollie: Do you want to do something tonight?

Ollie: I could pick you up.

Me: I'm sorry, I'm busy tonight.

Ollie: Doing what?

I put my phone on Do Not Disturb, opting not to reply.

"Do I look ok?" I ask the girls as I try on the fifteenth outfit.

"Yes," Sam says first.

"I told you four outfits ago that you found THE ONE," Chloe says, shaking her head.

"You said that to shut me up." I blink. "If you don't help me, I promise you, I will make you both sit there for another hour whilst I try them on all over again."

They both groan.

"Fine," Chloe responds. "But make sure you change your panties. I don't think you'll get any action wearing your Bridget Jones ones."

A laugh rips through me.

Lifting the shorts, I reveal my beige granny pants. "So, I shouldn't wear these?"

Her mouth drops open in shock. "God no. Throw them away right now."

"He might be into the old granny panties," Sam says seriously. "You never know, some men are into some crazy shit."

My laugh dies in my throat.

No, Chloe's right. There is no way Dominic will see me in anything other than sexy underwear. I would die of embarrassment if he ever caught me in these.

"Right, I'm going to try that outfit on one last time," I say over my shoulder as I head back into my room, tugging off the clothes and grabbing the pink co-ord set I stole off Chloe—a tiered skirt with a matching top fastened up the front with three bows.

I check myself in the mirror one last time.

"Chloe," I shout, and she pokes her head around my door. "Please fix my braid."

She huffs before coming to the rescue. "I told you to be careful!"

She has been my angel tonight, styling my hair into a loose braid and adding little diamantes through it, so it will sparkle every time the light hits.

After adding some white sandals and a matching bag, I blow them both a kiss as I jump into the taxi and head to Dominic's penthouse in Knightsbridge.

The closer I get, the streets bustling with expensive cars and lined with tall, elegant buildings, the more the nerves settle in.

Dominic opens the door as soon as the taxi comes to a stop outside his building.

"Hey, Shortcake." He leans down, pressing a kiss to my cheek, before paying the taxi driver and shutting the door. "You look beautiful." His eyes sweep over me for a second before he grasps my hand and tugs me inside, nodding at the security as we pass.

We enter the lift, and Dominic presses the button for the penthouse, adding his security code.

"Grace is here, but she'll be leaving soon," he says, his hand in mine.

"Who's Grace?"

I didn't know he had company. *God, I wish I had worn the black dress.*

"Grace is my friend, housekeeper, boss ... you name it." Dominic chuckles softly, and my shoulders instantly relax. "You'll adore her."

The lift comes to a stop, and the doors open. As soon as Dom unlocks his front door, Buddy comes barrelling towards us, barking like crazy.

"Hey Buddy." I scoop him into my arms and pepper his head with kisses.

"He missed you." Dominic's eyes soften as he watches us.

I swallow at the heat of his gaze. Buddy nuzzles against me, struggling to get as close as possible.

Dominic smiles.

"There you are!" a lady's voice says, and my head whips in the direction.

Making her way towards us is a beautiful, older woman, possibly in her fifties. Her smile is warm and welcoming as she reaches us. Her eyes narrow on Buddy, and his ears twitch.

"Listen here, Buddy. If you do your business one more time on that white rug, I will stop treats for a week!"

His ears drop as if he understands every word, his legs pushing at my chest as he wiggles to get down. I place him on the floor, and he rushes to her feet, pawing at her leg.

Her eyes soften as she rubs behind his ears. "He knows I can't be mad at him." She chuckles as she stands to her full height. "Sorry." She brushes her hands down her legs. "I'm Grace, and you must be Isabella. Nico didn't tell me exactly how beautiful you are."

Heat rushes to my cheeks.

She's the beautiful one. Her hair is tied neatly into a bun, her black-rimmed glasses sit perched on top of her head, and her smile is infectious. She makes me feel at home instantly.

"It's hard to describe such beauty," Dominic says before he leaves us, heading into the kitchen, Buddy hot on his heels.

"Right, sweetie." She pats my hand as she makes her way over to the door, grabbing her bag and coat off the hook. "I'll leave you to it."

"Are you not joining us?" I blurt out as I follow her.

"No," she says, smiling. "I thought it would be nice for you and Nico to eat alone tonight."

"Oh." My smile falls. "It's not a date." I look down at my feet. "Nancy is joining us."

"Nancy?" Grace doesn't hide her shock.

"Yeah, she's having a hard time. I thought I should invite her. You know, take her mind off things."

Grace hums before placing her things back on the hook. She links her arm through mine and steers us towards the kitchen. "Looks like I'm going to be enjoying this curry that Nico has been slaving over, after all."

Dominic's head lifts as we enter, his eyes on Grace, a smirk covering his face.

"I'll set another place," he says simply as he starts grabbing things out of the cupboard.

"Take a seat, sweetie." Grace unhooks her arm from mine, gesturing to the stools at the kitchen island. "I'll pour us some drinks, and we can watch the man at work."

I chuckle softly.

Dominic strokes my arm as he passes.

"Wait," Dominic says as he reaches inside the fridge and retrieves a strawberry daiquiri, placing it in front of me.

My eyes light up. He's even added sugar around the rim, a strawberry cut, sitting on the rim also. "You made me this?"

"Yes," he says, a slight blush touching his cheeks. "I've been practising, so don't complain if it isn't as nice as you would get at a bar."

I pick it up and take a sip. The mixture of the sweetness from the sugar and the sourness from the rum slides effortlessly down my throat. "No, it's good," I say with a smile.

His eyes darken as he stares at my lips. I swallow.

Leaning forward, he brushes the sugar from the side of my lip before sucking it off his finger.

And it's like everything else around me stops. My eyes are solely focused on his finger in his mouth, his soft lips wrapping around it as he sucks off the sugar.

"So, tell me about you. I only know the basics from Dominic," Grace says, drawing my attention away.

"There isn't much to tell, really." I shrug as I play with the steam on my glass. "I'm a waitress, an aspiring artist ... what else?" I tap my glass as I think. I hate the question. *What do you want to know? How deep are we going?*

"An aspiring artist?" Her eyes widen.

I nod.

"Wow, that's amazing, Bella. Maybe you could sell some of your pieces to this grump here." She flicks her head towards Dom. "This place could do with some brightening up."

"Grump?" He scoffs as he places his hands on the island, a smile curving at his lips. "There's no point; I'm hardly ever here."

"That's because he's always at the office." She shakes her head at him before glancing at me. "Hopefully that will be changing now."

My mouth snaps shut. *Will it?*

She pats my hand.

"So, what time is Nancy coming?"

Dominic's smile falls as he checks his watch. "Anytime now. I forgot to mention—I invited Kington as well."

The air changes quickly as Dominic's shoulders tense.

“He’s a good boy,” Grace mutters, her eyes flicking to me. “Kingston is a dreamboat. Wait until you meet him.”

I chuckle softly as she fans herself with her hand.

“Gracey,” Dominic says in a clipped tone.

“Oh, Nico, are you jealous?” She laughs. “I never thought I’d see the day.”

He shoots her a look.

“Oh, Nico.” Dom grabs some plates of food and heads to the table. “You know Isabella won't be interested ... anyway, we can window shop,” she adds, sending me a wink as a low growl slips past Dom’s lips, and I fight the urge to laugh.

He’s cute when he’s jealous.

But now, I really want to meet Kingston.

“Anyway ... Bella. How is that brother of yours?”

I frown. How does she know about Jason?

Noticing my frown, she explains, “Nico told me. I hope you don’t mind.”

“No, it's fine.”

I glance at Dominic, whose back is to me, setting the table. A bouquet of red roses sits in the middle as the flicker of candles dances around the room, covering each surface.

“What's wrong?” Dominic asks as he stops in front of me.

I shake my head. “Nothing.” I give him my best smile, hoping he believes it.

Pressing his knuckles under my chin, he lifts it so we're eye level. "Don't lie to me, Isabella."

"I think it's my fault," Grace offers. Dominic glances her way. "I mentioned her brother."

A buzzing sound cuts across us. "I'll get that." Grace jumps up, pressing the intercom.

"Hello, Miss Grace," a guy says. "There's a Miss Nancy and Mr. Kingston here."

"Thank you, Charles. I'll come down and get them," Grace says, turning to face us. "I'll give you two a minute."

She rushes out, shutting the door behind her, leaving Dominic and me alone.

I turn to face him.

He sighs. "Look, I didn't want to say anything until later." He rests his hands on the island as he looks at me. "But I went and visited your brother earlier this week." My eyes widen as he continues. "I told him that I'll be taking on his case."

I remain silent, motionless, as I let his words sink in.

"I'm going to work my ass off to get him out, Isabella."

I trace my fingertip around the brim of my glass, gathering all the sugar on my finger.

His eyes follow the movement as I feel his breath fanning across my cheek, his forearms flexing against the arms of my stool. His spicy aftershave hits me, and I inhale it, letting it wash over me.

Reaching forward, his strong hand clasps around my wrist as he pulls it towards his face, sucking my finger into his mouth as he stares intensely into my eyes.

My breath hitches.

Holy mother of ...

His tongue swirls slowly around my finger. The sexual tension in the air rips through me as a bead of sweat appears on my forehead, a tight curl sticking to it.

He finally releases it with a pop, his eyes darkening around the edges. His light blue eyes turn a darker shade as his lips curve into a smile, his hands caging me against the kitchen island. "Tastes so fucking sweet, Shortcake. But something tells me you taste even sweeter."

I blink, and before I have a chance to take my next breath, his lips slam against mine. I sit frozen for a second before I kiss him back, trying to take a little bit of control, but he doesn't allow it.

His tongue brushes against mine, and a moan slips free. He smiles against my lips as I tangle my hands in his hair and tug him closer to me, his body pressing mine against the counter.

The only sound is from the soft music playing and my heart pounding in my ears.

Someone clears their throat, and I freeze.

Busted.

Dominic tenses for a moment before he pulls back. His hands don't release me as his eyes darken, dropping down to my red, swollen lips.

I can't help but smile. The electricity between us is something I have never felt ... read about, yes ... but never experienced.

"Hi," Nancy mutters quietly from the front door, a bottle of champagne in her hands, and I'm instantly brought back to reality as I shrug off Dominic's hands. He rounds the island and begins dishing up the food.

"Nancy, hi," I say, clearing my throat as I try to control my racing heart.

Her brows tug together as she shrugs off her coat, hanging it on the hook. "I bought us a bottle," she says her eyes flick down to our daiquiris, and a frown appears on her face.

"I'm fine for now," I reply, gesturing to my half-empty glass.

"I'm fine too," Grace responds as she takes a sip of her wine.

"Nico?" Nancy asks, but he shakes his head. "Kingston?"

My eyes land on a tall, built guy, a formal black suit fitted to his broad shoulders, his piercing blue eyes on mine as if he's trying to read me. "No thanks, Nancy."

A smile touches his lips as he strides forwards, holding out his hand. "Hello, nice to finally meet you. I'm Kingston."

Ok, Grace is right. He is a dreamboat.

"Hi," I squeak as I place my hand in his.

Wow, where have all these hot men been hiding?

First Dominic, then Joey, now Kingston. Wait until my girls meet him; it will be a fight to the death.

"Hi," Dominic says in a gruff tone, his eyes narrowed at Kingston.

"How are you, Nancy?" I ask as she stands awkwardly next to the counter. Dominic pours her a small glass of champagne, but she takes the bottle from him and fills it to the brim.

"I'm fine," she answers, her eyes focused on Dominic. "Are you cooking?"

"I am."

She clears her throat, her eyes finding their way to mine. "I never thought I'd see the day."

A shadow passes across her face. Picking up the glass and the bottle, she spins on her heels, dropping down into a chair at the table.

Chapter 24

Dominic

I've never planned on killing a detective before, but watching Kingston shake Isabella's hand, and how she smiled up at him ... it awakened a beast inside of me that's clawing to get out.

I sit here, tucking into my food as I listen to Kingston fire questions at my girl.

"So, your friends—they live with you?"

"Yes." She smiles sweetly, like he isn't interrogating her.

Can I be jealous that she's only smiling at him? Fuck, I'm in deep.

"We met at Wilson's and immediately hit it off."

Kingston nods, hanging onto her every word.

"I couldn't do life without them, if I'm honest. They're amazing." She shoots me a smile. "So, Kingston, tell me about you?"

"There isn't much to tell," he says.

Kingston is a closed book; no matter how hard you probe, you will never get the answers you want out of him.

He is a mystery.

"Do you have a girlfriend?"

He shakes his head.

"Do you want a girlfriend?"

He shakes his head again.

"Do you want to be here?"

A laugh bursts from him.

A smile tugs at my lips.

"I was just checking you were paying attention." Isabella chuckles. "But seriously, there isn't any Mrs Kingston? You see, I'm asking for a friend ..."

My head whips in her direction, and I notice she's wiggling her brows at Grace, who bats her off.

"I'll take Gracey out any time she wants for dinner; she only has to give me the nod." Kingston shoots Grace a wink, and her cheeks instantly begin to redden.

Nancy has barely said a word throughout the evening, her eyes focused solely on her glass. The once-full bottle is now nearly empty.

"Nancy, are you ok?"

She pushes her food around her plate. "Just got a lot on my mind, is all."

"Have you received any more notes?" Isabella asks her.

She sighs, then reaches into her bag and places some slips of paper in the middle of the table.

Eight pieces of paper, to be exact.

"Nancy, I'm going to need those for evidence," Kingston says, narrowing his eyes. "From now on, you need to call me as soon as possible. I won't get any fingerprints on them now."

"I'm sorry," Nancy says as she swallows. "Here, take them," she adds as she pushes the crumbled papers towards him.

"Thanks. I'll get Blue onto them as soon as I head into the office tomorrow," he says, placing the notes into evidence bags and tucking them into his pocket.

I zone out as Isabella and Grace begin speaking about a TV programme called *The Vampire Diaries.*

Isabella fits perfectly into my life; she's funny, calm, and a little chaotic.

I've watched her spill her daiquiri down her chin three times tonight.

My eyes drift to Nancy.

Her normal impeccable demeanour is gone, replaced with something else.

She's anxious, and she has every fucking right to be.

"Dom, are you ok?" Isabella asks as she places her hand in mine, and I interlock our fingers, bringing her hand to my mouth.

"I'm fine, Shortcake."

A smile touches her lips as I press a lingering kiss on her hand.

"Nancy, have you thought about moving out for a while? Maybe staying somewhere safe, instead of your townhouse?" Kingston asks.

Nancy's eyes swing in his direction. "No, I'll be fine. I won't have anyone draw me out of the home I have made."

"I think you should consider it. Even if just in the short term."

"I think Kingston is right," Isabella says, her hand flexing in mine as I squeeze it.

"I've been through a lot in my life, Isabella," Nancy says. "I won't let this affect me. I can't." A shadow passes over her face as she picks up her glass and finishes the contents. "Anyways, this has been lovely. Thank you so much for inviting me. I needed it," she says, smiling at me before she pushes her chair out and makes her way towards the front door, grabbing her things. "But I have a meeting first thing, and I need to prep."

"Wait, Nancy," Grace says as she jumps up. "I'll walk out with you."

"Kingston, a word in my office, before you head out?" I say to Kingston, who nods, grabbing his things and heading towards the corridor.

Isabella begins to rise, but my hand squeezes hers tight, stopping her. Her eyes land on mine. "Wait here until I'm done?"

She nods, and I press a quick kiss to her forehead.

Having an office in my home has become more helpful than not.

Kingston stands by the window, whiskey in hand—apparently having helped himself to my decanter—staring down at the bustling streets below.

"Thanks for hanging back," I say, dropping into the chair behind my desk.

"Take a seat," I say, motioning to the empty chair opposite. "I just wanted to thank you for coming tonight."

"Care to tell me why I was really invited?"

"Fine, you got me," I say, clasping my hands in front of me. "It seems Giovanni is on something of a rampage as of late."

Kingston sighs.

He knows this means more of a "clean-up" for him.

"And what do you expect me to do about it?" he says, crossing one leg over the other.

"I think it's in the best interest of everyone if there are a few more police on the streets in the next few weeks," I say, arching my eyebrow.

"Consider it done," he says as he stands, his fingers tracing down the buttons on his blazer. "How are things with Isabella?"

I frown. "What's that any business of yours?"

"She's good for you. She's smart, driven, beautiful—"

A growl involuntarily slips past my lips.

"Calm down, big guy," he says, straightening his black tie. "Isabella is all of those things, but I can tell you right now, she's all those things for *you*. Not me," he says. "I'll be in contact over the next few days concerning Nancy."

Chapter 25

Isabella

Sam: Tell me you're staying the night.

Chloe: Of course she fucking is! Did you see the underwear she's wearing?

Sam: Booyah! *Dancing emoji*

Sam: It's about God damn time, my babe! Lie back and think of bloody England.

Chloe: I don't think she will have time to think of England, you doughnut!

Sam: You never know … just because he is hot as fuck, doesn't automatically mean the man is skilled in the bedroom.

Chloe: Oh, please, lord, let that man be skilled. *praying hand emoji* Our girl deserves it!

"You're not leaving, are you?" Dominic says behind me as I take my coat off the hook.

"I was going to, yeah."

He stops in front of me. "We haven't even had dessert."

His words drip over me. My eyes flick to his, and I see the heat in them. He smirks as his fingers wrap around my coat, tugging it from me, and he hangs it back on the hook.

His warm, strong hand presses against my lower back as he steers me further into his apartment before opening the door to his bedroom.

My jaw drops.

The curtains are closed, and soft, dim lights fill the space.

There's a hint of vanilla around the room from the candles scattered on every side. Red rose petals cover the floor, and there's a plate on the centre of the coffee table, containing broken pieces of chocolate.

"How did you know?" I smile as my eyes fix on the chocolate.

"I asked your friends," he says, tucking a piece of hair behind my ear that has fallen from the braid. "They said your favourite chocolate was broken pieces of dairy milk, so I grabbed two big bars." He bends down, his lips brushing my ear as he lowers his voice. "The other one is in the fridge."

I swallow. *Quit talking dirty to me, Dom.*

His fingers wrap around mine as he tugs me to the sofa.

"Have you had a good night?" he asks as I relax against him, our fingers interlocking.

"I did. The food was delicious; you outdid yourself."

"I'm glad you enjoyed it." His muscles tense behind me. "I was wondering ..."

I hear the rare nervousness return to his voice.

"Would you like to stay over?"

My head whips around as I stare into his eyes. "You want me to stay?"

"Yeah." He chuckles softly, "I mean, I have four bedrooms. You can stay in one of those. Unless ..."

He leaves the unsaid words hanging in the air.

I tug my bottom lip between my teeth.

"Four bedrooms?" I ask.

Dominic nods.

"I guess I could stay ... but I don't want to sleep alone."

As soon as the words leave my mouth, Dominic moves from behind me. He tugs at my braid, and my hair falls free. "I like your curls," he says, stroking my face as he climbs to his knees in front of me, picking up a piece of chocolate and holding it towards my lips. "Open up for me, baby."

My mouth drops open as I take it from him, his eyes never wavering from mine.

"You are so beautiful," he whispers as his lips graze my jaw. My pulse jumps as he peppers kisses down my neck to my collarbone before repeating the action.

His lips brush mine like a feather; my heart beats wildly.

I groan against him as he trails light kisses alongside my jaw once more.

I want to scream in frustration.

He smiles against me, his lips brushing my skin with every word. "Do you want me to kiss you again, Shortcake?"

I nod, goosebumps dancing along my skin.

I want to tangle my hands in his hair and tug his lips to mine. To kiss him fiercely. But I don't.

His eyes finally find mine, and he gives me what I need.

The moment his mouth brushes mine, I know I'm lost.

He has me.

And that scares the ever-loving shit out of me.

He rests between my thighs. "Tell me to stop," he whispers against my lips as he pushes me back onto the sofa, leaning above me. I taste the chocolate on his tongue, and a small moan slips past my lips.

"I don't want you to stop," I say breathlessly. My skin ignites with every touch.

I couldn't stop him, even if I wanted to.

And my God, I don't want him to.

I wrap my hands around his arms. "Please, Dom. Don't stop."

His eyes flare as he leans above me, fingertips gliding down my chest as they reach the first bow on my top. "This has been torturing me all night ..." His hand tugs at the first bow, and it unravels, revealing my light pink lace bra.

My breath hitches as his eyes darken more, and a low growl leaves his lips.

He wastes no time moving to the next bow, unravelling it. "Shortcake, are you wearing a matching set?"

I nod, unable to form a single word.

"Fuck." He groans, the vein in his neck standing to attention. He moves to the next, and once he's unravelled all the strings, the top falls slightly. His tongue darts out, wetting his lips, as he brushes his nose against my nipple, the friction making my eyes squeeze shut. "Do you want my mouth on you first?" His breath fans across my skin.

I nod.

His lips wrap around my nipple, sucking it hard. Using his other hand, he palms the other.

"Dom." I moan as he switches between them.

He trails kisses down my stomach as he reaches the brim of my skirt. His hands stroke up my thighs before they reach my pink panties. "I need these off." He growls as he tugs them off, along with my skirt, leaving me bare to him. "The need to taste you has overcome me ... buried itself deep inside me," he whispers against my heat. “I can smell how wet you are for me, Shortcake.” His hand brushes against me, and I hiss.

This is the first time I’ve been touched in a long time, and my entire body feels sensitive, like I may combust at any moment.

He parts my folds, his thumb brushing my clit, and a wave of pleasure hits. “Don’t close those pretty blue eyes, Shortcake. I need you to watch me as I devour you.”

My eyes snap open, clashing with his, as I watch his tongue dart out as it brushes against me. His mouth latches onto my clit, and his fingers brush against my entrance before he pushes them slowly inside me, filling me.

“Holy fuck.” I cry out from the sensation.

I’ve never felt so alive as I do with him.

His mouth, his hand, fuck ... can I sign up for this every night?

He tears his mouth away from me. I want to scream, to tell him I’m close, but no words leave me as his fingers continue their steady assault.

“Tell me, Shortcake, do you think of me when you touch yourself?” His hand pauses its movements as he waits for my reply.

I nod.

“Fuck,” he breathes out, rubbing the pad of his thumb over my swollen clit. “I want to see what you do to yourself, whilst you think of me.”

My eyes snap open. I shake my head as I try to close my thighs, but his hand jolts out and stops me.

"Isabella," he says, his eyes softening.

I freeze for a moment, searching his face.

I've never felt confident in my life, ever. Not growing up. Not with Myles. But Dominic makes my whole body feel alive.

I let out a breath as I give myself a small pep talk, before slowly gliding my hand down my body and pushing it between my thighs. A low rumble comes from Dominic, and my eyes snap to his, the moment I touch myself. I moan as I feel how wet I am.

How wet I am for him.

"Fuck this," he rushes out. I squeal as he lifts me over his shoulder and strides towards the bed, dropping me onto it.

He slowly undoes the buttons on his shirt, slipping it off and throwing it onto the chair in the corner. "Christ, Shortcake. You're so fucking perfect. And you're all mine."

My mouth waters as he continues to shed his clothes until he's standing completely naked in front of me, his thick cock standing to attention. Reaching into the bedside table, he pulls out a condom, and he tears the packet open with his teeth. "Are you on birth control?"

I shake my head.

"Fuck." He groans as his hand squeezes the condom packet in his hand. "I can't wait to feel you one day. To feel nothing between us."

My eyes lock onto his cock as he wraps his hand around himself, slowly dragging the condom onto his cock.

I expect him to climb up the bed and lean above me, but he shocks me as he wraps his hand around my ankle and yanks me down.

"You're mine, from this point forward."

He lines himself up with my entrance, pushing in inch by inch.

"You."

Thrust.

"Are."

Thrust.

"Mine."

My breath leaves me in a whoosh as he picks up his pace.

"Dom," I whisper as my hands squeeze his arms tight, my nails digging into his skin.

A shudder runs down his body as he leans close, his mouth latching onto my neck.

He thrusts into me again and again, until a shiver of pleasure runs through me, and I throw my head back, a moan ripping through me as he seals it with a kiss.

His cock jerks inside me as he tears his mouth from mine, burying it into my neck.

"Fuck."

Buddy jumps over me excitedly as I wake, finding the bed otherwise empty. "Good morning, Buddy," I say as I pull him off me and tuck him into my side.

He snuggles against me as I wrap Dominic's plush duvet around us, sinking further into his memory foam mattress. It's like sleeping on a cloud.

The light from the blinds seeps through as I look around the room. It's probably the size of my whole apartment. His sides are clean, not a speck of dust on them, whereas mine have cups that have been sitting there for days and a huge pile of laundry sitting in the corner, waiting for me to tackle it.

"Good morning, Shortcake," Dominic says as he enters the room. His hair is wet from his shower. He's already in his suit, ready for the day.

"Good morning," I whisper back, pulling the duvet tighter around me.

He stops right in front of me as he sits on the bed, his eyes focusing on the little lump in the duvet as he pulls it back, revealing Buddy. His brow raises. "He's not allowed in the bedroom ... let alone the bed," he says, a smile threatening to tug at his lips.

"But he is so happy here," I coo as I tug Buddy tighter.

His nose twitches as his eyes snap open and land on Dominic. His eyes snap up, and his bum shakes excitedly as he climbs out of my embrace and rushes to his daddy.

"Once you're ready, I've made you a sandwich and a cup of tea. I'll drop you home on my way to work," Dominic says, pulling my eyes to his.

"Oh. Thanks," I mumble as I sit up, pulling the blanket tighter around me.

"Hey," he says, leaning close to me, gripping my chin. "I have an important meeting that I can't cancel ... otherwise, I would have spent the day with you." His eyes search mine.

I nod. "No, I know," I say, clearing my throat. "I have work as well, so please, don't worry."

He lets out a breath, his hand falling. "I enjoyed every minute of last night." A smirk covers his face as his eyes drop down my body. "And I meant what I said, Shortcake. You are mine."

His words vibrate through me.

"What about if I don't want to be?" I tease.

He jumps forward, and I fall back as he leans above me, the blanket falling to bare my breasts. I try to cover them, but he stops me. "Maybe I need to remind you how good it feels ..."

Chapter 26

Dominic - Age 13

"Gio, stop!" I yell loudly as I'm pulled back against my father's chest, his arms wrapped tightly around me to stop me from pulling away.

Giovanni continues to punch the lifeless boy on the floor.

"Don't," my father says in my ear as I struggle to get free.

Why is he doing this? I want to scream, but I know there's no point.

At first, the kid gave as good as he got, landing a few punches on Giovanni—but he was no match in the end.

Giovanni's eyes are misted over as he continues, not stopping for a breath, his dark hair clinging to the sweat on his forehead.

I notice a few kids from our school standing to the side, not tearing their eyes away from the scene in front of us, but no one dares to stop it.

Roberto had his security deal with anyone who tried.

Giovanni's chest rises and falls as he tries to control his breathing.

“Gio?” I say. His eyes snap to mine, the mist clearing from them. and his bottom lip begins to shake. “Come here,” I say, holding out my hand towards him, but he shakes his head.

“Dad, let me go.” My father tenses behind me but reluctantly pulls his arms away. “Don’t get involved,” he warns me as he levels his eyes with mine.

“Is he ...” I motion towards the kid lying lifelessly on the floor.

My dad follows my eyeline, his shoulders drop, and he nods.

My breath leaves me in a whoosh.

My eyes snap back to Giovanni, who stares blankly at the boy on the floor once more, his hands shaking by his sides.

“Gio?” I say quietly as I take a step closer to him, and his eyes snap to mine again.

Regret. That’s what I see written across his face.

“Nico,” he says quietly as he takes a hesitant step towards me. “I couldn’t—"

“My boy!” Roberto says with pride as he cuts across me, wrapping his arm around his shoulders and tugging him to his side.

Giovanni masks his features immediately.

“Finally, I see me in you,” he says proudly as he stands in front of Giovanni, “rather than the weakness of your father,” he spits. Giovanni's shoulders tense, but he remains quiet.

And at that exact moment, the life I once saw in Giovanni's eyes disappears.

It's a light that never comes back.

Chapter 27

Dominic

"Nancy," I say, as I spot her sitting in my office waiting for me.

She chews on her nail, something she does when she has things on her mind.

"Nico, hey," she says, a crease appearing on her forehead. "I hope you don't mind me ambushing you first thing."

"Not at all," I reply as I make my way to my desk and take a seat. "What's wrong?"

"When I got home last night, something didn't feel ... right," she says quietly as she takes a seat opposite me, her hands wrapped tightly in her lap. "And then when I got into my room ..." Her voice cracks. "Someone had been inside my apartment, and they'd cut up all my clothes." A tear streaks down her cheek.

My hand pauses on my keyboard, and I lift my head. "What did you just say?"

Did I hear her correctly? Someone was in her apartment?

"Why didn't you call me?"

She sighs. "They weren't there anymore. It didn't seem pressing."

"You always call me," I snap. Her eyes widen, and I let out a breath, softening my approach. "It doesn't matter what time of day. I promised your father I would look out for you."

Her shoulders rise and fall as she lets out a breath. "Enough!" she hisses, and I slam my mouth closed. "I'm fed up with you saying you only look out for me because of my father."

"Nancy;" I sigh. "We've gone over this."

"I know." She slams her hands on my desk, making the contents rattle. "Fuck, Nico ..." She drops her face into her hands. "It's not you, and I'm so sorry for dropping these problems on you, but you're the person I always run to."

I keep quiet.

"What would they have done if I were there? Would they have hurt me? Nico, Kingston was right. I can't go home ..." She cries harder, twisting in her seat. Her hands wrap around mine. “Please, can I stay with you? I promise you won't know I’m there.”

Her watery eyes search mine as she waits for my answer.

Her father would be turning in his grave if he knew I’d taken my eye off the ball.

I reluctantly nod, hoping I won’t regret this.

Chapter 28

Isabella

Ollie: Isabella, this is the longest we haven't spoken since we met.

Ollie: Call me.

Ollie: I came by Wilson's, but you were too busy speaking to your friends. I'll come see you another day.

Ollie: Do you not miss me?

"I may need to head home. My bloody grandma is being a nightmare." Sam scrunches up her face as she continues. "I had a call from her local police department ... apparently she was running through the street last night, sleepwalking." A laugh rips through me as Sam tells us about the adventures of her grandmother.

"It's not funny," Sam mutters solemnly, shaking her head. "She was naked."

I burst out laughing, the contents of the cup of tea spitting all over the counter.

Over the years, Sam has told us many stories of Grandma Violet, and she sounds like a hoot.

"You wouldn't say that if you knew her," Sam says, shaking her head.

"We need to meet her," Chloe adds. "Imagine taking her out ... hey! I bet she would get more numbers than us all." She shoots me a look.

Sam has always kept us separate from her family, never explaining to us why, and we never push her. We all have our secrets, and that's fine.

"Please ... there will be no competition."

"When will you need to head home?" I ask, not wanting Sam to leave. Last time she was gone weeks.

"I don't know." She shrugs, a shadow passing across her face. "Maybe next week. It all depends on my mother."

"What do you mean?"

"Ladies." Dominic's voice sounds behind me, and we all whip around.

"Hey," I say, smiling as I lean over the counter and press a quick kiss to his lips. "What's wrong?" I ask as I search his face.

It's like he has the weight of the world on his shoulders.

"Can we talk?" He motions with his head to the side.

My smile falls as I follow him. He walks up towards the back table as we take a seat.

My hands wrap together in my lap, my shoulders tensing, and I bite my bottom lip.

He clasps his hands together on the table. "When I got to work this morning, Nancy was waiting for me in my office." I sit quietly as he continues. "Fuck, Bel. The fucker was in her apartment last night."

My jaw drops open. "What? Is she ok?"

He nods. "She doesn't want to spend indefinite time in a hotel, and it's not safe for her to go home …" He pauses, his words sinking in. "So, I've said she can stay with me. Temporarily."

I remain silent. No words, no movements, nothing, all my insecurities bubbling to the surface.

"Shortcake?" Dominic's voice draws me out of my trance. "Look, this doesn't change anything. We have a history, yes, but she's just a colleague and an old friend. That's it. Nothing will happen, I promise you."

He holds out his hand on the table, and I look down at it but make no effort to move.

He sighs, dragging his hand through his hair. "I couldn't send her back home."

I see the war going on inside his head, and I want to comfort him, to tell him that everything's fine and that I trust him ...

But I also trusted Myles, and look where that got me.

"I understand." I lean forward, squeezing his hand briefly before pulling back. "I've got to get back to work."

His eyes search mine, his shoulders dropping. "Well, I'll have my usual."

I nod, jumping up and rushing into the kitchen, my eyes stinging.

I avoid looking at anyone as I pass, but I feel their eyes on me.

"What's going on?" Georgina asks as she looks up from the sink. She asked to help Manny in the kitchen today; she wants to learn how to cook, so she came in on her day off.

"Nothing. Everything," I say, shrugging as I jump up and sit on the counter.

She sits next to me as she dries her hands with the towel. "Who's upset you? I've been learning a lot of new tricks lately. You know, if you put eye drops in someone's coffee, they have the shits for hours ..." She gives me a look, and a chuckle slips free. "Because gimme the nod, baby girl, and I'll do it now. I'm sure I have some in my bag somewhere." She goes to jump off the counter, but my hand jolts out, stopping her.

"It's not important," I say, shrugging.

She shoots me a look.

"Fine." I sigh. "It's Dominic. His colleague is moving in with him indefinitely." Georgina's hands flex on the towel, but she remains silent, letting me continue. "I know I shouldn't feel this way, but they were sleeping together, before me ..."

"Before you?" she interjects, and I nod.

"I know what you're going to say ... to trust him, because he hasn't done anything to make me not believe him. But it's hard when the only partner you've ever had cheats on you, and then you meet this incredible guy ..." I sigh, thinking of how amazing Dominic actually is. He has been nothing but charming to me, treating me perfectly. Looking after Buddy, even though I can tell he didn't want to.

"I don't think you should tarnish every guy with the same brush as your ex, because your ex was a little shit."

I laugh. That's putting it mildly.

She continues. "Now, obviously, I don't know Dominic personally." She clears her throat. "But from what you've said, he seems a decent enough guy."

I remain silent, watching our feet dangle.

"She's right, sweetie," Phoebe says as she leans against the cabinet opposite, clearly having been listening from outside. "Give Dominic a chance. Don't let something pass you by that could turn out to be amazing."

I let their words sink in.

I know they're definitely right about one thing: I shouldn't tarnish everyone with the same brush as Myles.

"Right, I have some paperwork to go through," Phoebe says, pushing off the counter. "Bella, come find me before you finish today." She turns and heads out of the kitchen.

Georgina turns to me. "Please, see what happens. Speak to him." She shoots me a look before jumping off the counter.

"Hey, kid," Manny says behind me. "Table three's order is ready." His eyes search my face. "Do you want me to take it?"

"No," I say, shaking my head as I get down off the counter and take the plate from him. "It's fine."

I push open the door, walking through the restaurant, and stop right in front of Dominic.

I place the plate down in front of him, and his head snaps up. "Shortcake ..."

"No, wait," I say, cutting him off as I sit opposite him. I need to get my words out before I lose the confidence to say them. "I'm sorry for storming off, but my ex, Myles, cheated on me, and ever since, I feel like I'm constantly expecting the other shoe to drop. I have to trust that you are not the same. That that won't happen. That this is real."

He leans across the table, grasping my hand and pressing a kiss to my knuckles.

My hard exterior is melting into a puddle at my feet.

God, how does he do that?

"Baby, nothing would make me want to risk this. What time do you finish?" he asks. "I'd like to take you out to dinner."

I look at the clock behind me. "I still have four hours."

"That's fine, I'll wait," he says, pulling out his laptop.

I take the opportunity to see what Phoebe wanted to talk about.

"There you are," she says as she leans back in her chair, placing a half-eaten slice of cake back on its plate.

"Has something happened?"

She lets out a breath. "Promise you won't be mad."

"What is it?" My shoulders drop as I sigh.

She turns the screen slowly towards me, and my eyes land on it.

"What is—" The words die in my mouth as my eyes flicker across the screen. "You're buying lights?" My brows pinch together.

"Yes," she says quickly. "It's for your exhibition."

My mouth drops open.

"Sam told me about finding your art ..." She pauses for a minute, her hand playing with the keyboard. "Now, I know you don't want people sticking their nose into your business, but I've been thinking about it for a while now, and I think if you just focus on your art and leave the rest up to us ... we could really pull something special off."

I knew Sam wouldn't be able to keep her mouth shut.

"I can't let you close this place for the evening," I say, my eyes flickering around her office.

"You can and you will." She sighs. "I'm sure Sam knows a lot of influencers that would jump at the chance to come to something like this ..."

I shoot her a look. Is she joking?

"Everything helps, and I know Sam has been messaging as many people as possible. We will sort this, Isabella." She says, squeezing my hand on the table. "Give us a few weeks, and we will have the best event this side of London has ever seen."

Chapter 29

Dominic

Giovanni: Alessandro is causing trouble.

Giovanni: Do I need to have a word?

Me: Leave Alessandro to me.

"Finally, I get you alone," a small voice says behind me, making me drop my phone to the table.

Standing next to my table is a beautiful older woman, maybe in her fifties. Her brown eyes focus on mine, and her lips turn up into a small smile.

"Calm yourself, big guy." She slaps me on the shoulder as she takes a seat in front of me. "I've been hearing a lot about you, and I wanted to meet you myself."

She's confident, and I like it.

A smile tugs at my lips as she motions with her hand to the girl behind the counter.

"Yes, Phoebes?" she says as she reaches us.

"Can we have two cups of tea, please, Angel?"

Angel's eyes flicker to mine, and she lingers for a few seconds before nodding and rushing away.

"So, Dominic," Phoebe says as she clasps her hands on the table in front of her. "Tell me about yourself. I know you're a lawyer. I know you have a lodger. Is there anything else?"

Lodger? Is that what we are calling Nancy these days?

"Seems you already know a lot about me," I say, raising an eyebrow.

She smirks. "Google tells you a lot."

A laugh rips through me at her bluntness. "I can see why Isabella likes you."

"Well, we love her like a daughter," she says, her smile falling as she turns serious. "So, just remember that before you break her heart, because you see that big guy over there?" I follow her eyeline to the older guy leaning against the doorframe, a frying pan in his hand, his glare fixed firmly on me. "He'll hurt you if you do."

I smile. "It's nice to see Isabella has a lot of people around her, who care for her."

She taps her hands against the table as she rises to her feet. "It was nice getting to know you, and I hope for Isabella's sake it works out between the two of you."

My voice halts her. "I'm thinking of taking Isabella away." She turns to face me. "She's going to need a week—actually, make it two—off work."

"When?"

"As soon as possible."

Phoebe remains silent for a few seconds. "Consider it approved."

"You sure I can't convince you to stay?" I whisper against Bella's neck, goosebumps appearing along her skin.

"No," she says breathlessly as she tilts her head to the side, and I pepper her delicate neck with kisses. Her soft moans fill my car as we sit outside her apartment. Her pulse quickens beneath my lips.

"Please, Shortcake." I smile against her as my hand drifts up her thigh until I reach her lace panties.

"Dom, you've got to stop," she says unconvincingly.

I can feel her need for me even through the fabric, and I slip them aside and glide my fingers between her wet folds.

Her head flies back, resting against the headrest as her eyes squeeze closed.

Her breath comes out low and hollow as she opens her thighs wider.

"Imagine if you came home with me ... how I could fuck you all night long," I whisper in her ear. A moan slips free as her walls clench tightly around my fingers.

My cock strains against my zipper as I adjust myself. Isabella's hand jolts out, pushing me away, as she strokes me over my trousers with her other one.

"Dom, I don't think we should be doing this ... here."

"Then stop me." I grip her chin and tilt her head to me, enjoying the flush of her cheeks, before I slam my lips against hers.

Her hand continues to stroke me over my trousers to the rhythm of my fingers inside of her.

"I can't—" She freezes as she tears her lips from mine, her head falling back against the headrest as I press my face into his neck. Her scent surrounds me as my own pleasure builds. She strokes me faster as she finds her own release, our heavy breathing mixing as I spill into my boxers.

"Fuck." I let out a chuckle.

She giggles as she adjusts her dress and turns to face me. "I need to go; the girls are waiting for me."

"Ok," I say, a wave of disappointment running through me. "I'll see you tomorrow?"

"Maybe," she says with a wink before pressing a quick kiss to my lips and jumping out.

I watch her let herself into her apartment before I head home.

Fuck.

I pinch the bridge of my nose the moment I open the front door and am confronted with a mountain of moving boxes.

How long is she staying for?

I need a stiff drink.

"Nancy," I shout as I shrug off my blazer and place it on my hook before heading in search of her.

My eyes land on the lit candles scattered around the open space and the takeaway bags on the island.

Nancy's back is to me as she stands in the kitchen, shaking Buddy off her leg. “Argh, will you just get down?” She sighs. “Nico, when are you getting rid of this dog?” The words die in her mouth as she turns and spots me behind her.

Buddy barks louder this time.

“Buddy,” I say, patting my leg, and he instantly rushes to my side, nudging my leg with his head as I bend and rub him behind the ear.

“Really, Nico,” she says, tutting. “An apartment isn’t a place for a dog.”

I ignore her as I open the cabinet and pour myself a whiskey before heading out to my wrap-around terrace, looking out over Knightsbridge.

I take a seat, stretching out my legs as I shrug off my tie, and throw it onto the table.

“You know, it's really beautiful here,” Nancy says as she takes a seat next to me.

It's dark out now; the lights illuminate the streets, and the soft glow from inside seeps out here.

“Nancy, we need to talk about those boxes.”

Her shoulders drop as she takes a big sip of her wine. “Before you say anything, Grace has already had a word with me.”

Thank God for Grace.

“I want to thank you for taking me in, looking after me,” she says as she places her legs next to mine on the table.

"I promised—"

"Don't say it again," she snaps, and I close my mouth. "I know you look after me because of my father, and I'm grateful ... but Nico, don't you do it because *you* care for me?"

And just like that, reality hits.

The reality that I am living with someone I used to fuck.

Someone I know has feelings for me.

Chapter 30

Isabella

Sam: You sure we can't convince you to come out with us?

Chloe: Please . . . we're sleeping at Beth's after?

Me: No, you girls go ahead. I'm still not feeling too great.

Sam: Babe, do you want us to come home and bring some chicken soup and nurse you back to health?

Me: Seriously, *rolling eye emoji* I don't even like chicken soup.

Chloe: It's what people bring, no?

Sam: Have a sleep and we will look after you tomorrow. Love you.

There's a soft knock at the door.

Who the hell is that?

"Coming," I say loudly as I pad towards it, checking the peephole.

Dominic.

Oh, God, what is he doing here?

Looking down at myself, I scrunch up my nose. Great, I'm wearing my oldest pyjamas, zero makeup, and don't get me started on my hair.

This is the first time I've had a cold in years, and all I want to do is sleep it off.

Opening the door, I spot Buddy tucked safely under Dominic's arm.

I reach for Buddy, and he licks me excitedly before I place him onto his paws, and he immediately rushes off to explore my place.

He's just as bad as I am for snooping.

"What are you doing here?" I ask, wrapping my oversized cardigan tightly around me.

"That's no way to greet your boyfriend," he says, an amused look in his eyes.

My mouth slams shut.

Boyfriend.

Holy shit ... a boyfriend! I haven't had a boyfriend since ... *no, don't go there again.*

Wipe that asshole from your memory.

He leans forward, wrapping his arm around my waist and tugging me into his chest. As he leans in for a kiss, I turn my head at the last second. His lips graze my cheek. "Why aren't you kissing me?" he asks, frowning.

"Because I'm poorly and gross," I say as I pull out of his embrace and plonk down on the sofa, covering myself with the blanket.

"I know," he says as he takes a seat on the coffee table. "So, I bought a care package."

"A what?"

He smirks as he reaches inside the paper bags at his feet. "Red roses"—he holds out the bunch, and I take them from him—"because I know they are your favourite. I also brought you chocolate, that I've already broken into pieces." He sends me a wink as he passes me a plastic container containing numerous pieces of broken diary milk. "Then, I got you some pyjamas." He passes me an oversized black T-shirt and joggers that are probably men's.

"Dom, I think you got me the wrong size," I say with a frown.

"No, these are my clothes," he says, lowering his voice as he reaches out and strokes my face. "I want you smelling of me when I'm not around."

A smile touches my lips as I wipe the tissue under my nose.

Buddy jumps up on the sofa, snuggling against me.

"And, well ..." He pauses for a second as I see a wave of uncertainty run across his face as he reaches inside the bag once more. "I noticed your bracelet," he says, flicking his chin down to my bracelet that Jason gave me, and my fingers automatically rub against the charms. "I wanted to get you something ..." He hands me a small pink box.

I sit up straight, opening it. My eyes land on a small strawberry charm. "Dom, it's beautiful," I breathe, brushing my fingertips over it.

"I can't look at a strawberry daiquiri now without thinking of the sugar on your lips," he says as his thumb brushes lightly against my bottom lip. "I want you to know how important you are to me, Shortcake."

Swoon.

He closes the distance, his lips brushing mine, and my body automatically moulds to his as I get lost in the kiss. Gentle, passionate.

Reaching up, I brush my hand against his stubble, and the moment his tongue brushes mine, I pull back, tearing my mouth from his. "Dom, I'm sick, and I don't want you to get it," I say, shaking my head.

I want nothing more than to get lost in him, but right now all I want is my bed and a hot cup of tea.

He nods before standing up, and a wave of disappointment rushes through me.

What do you expect? You've basically told him to go without actually showing him the door.

I gasp as he pulls back the blanket and lifts me effortlessly into his arms.

"Dom, what are you doing?" I let out a shriek, my arms wrapping tightly around his neck.

"You're sick, and I'm looking after you. Now, which one is your room?" he asks as he weaves through the mismatched furniture towards the corridor.

"Second on the left."

It's only a moment before he's kicking open my door and placing me gently onto the bed.

"Now, you get comfortable. I'm going to let Buddy out quickly and make you a cup of tea."

"You're coming back?" I don't hide the shock in my voice.

"Of course I'm coming back," he says as he leans down and brushes my hair off my forehead before placing the tissue box on the bed. "My girlfriend is sick. What kind of boyfriend would I be if I just left you to look after yourself?" He leaves his question hanging in the air.

Just like my last one.

"Now, I'll be back in a minute." He presses a kiss to my forehead before he disappears, and I hear the front door shut.

Oh my God. He's here—looking after me.

After a few minutes, Dominic comes back into the bedroom, carrying a cup of tea, and he places it on my bedside table.

Reaching out, he presses his hand against my forehead. "You're not too warm."

I nod.

This is the first time he's been in my room, and I'm disgusting.

"You've added the charm," he says, his thumb grazing over the strawberry as he sits on the edge of the bed.

"Of course I have. It's beautiful."

"Now I don't know the protocol for looking after a sick patient," he says, smirking as he takes off his tie and undoes the first buttons on his shirt. "But I know it's all about looking after you."

My breath catches as he tears back the blanket and takes a seat on the bed. His hand strokes up my bare thigh, causing goosebumps to dance along my skin, before his hand reaches the bottom of my shorts, and he pauses. "And, Shortcake, that's what I'm going to do."

He kneels between my thighs, pushing them apart and tugging my shorts and panties together down my legs. A wolfish smile covers his face as he stares down at my pussy. I gasp as his breath fans across my exposed clit.

"Dom, you don't—" I hiss as his tongue darts out, flicking lightly against my clit before he pulls back.

"It's all a part of the care package." He blows another stream of cool air onto my clit, and my hips buck off the bed. His hand jolts out, stopping me, and I frown. "Tell me if it's too much, and I'll stop and just cuddle you."

"Please, it's not enough," I practically whimper. I need his mouth on me more than I need my next breath.

Reaching beneath me, he drapes my thighs over his shoulders before he begins devouring me.

More. More.

I want to scream, but no words come out.

He's feasting on me like a starved man, and I'm enjoying every fucking second of it, my cold a distant thought.

My moans echo off the walls of my small bedroom, and I'm just glad my girls aren't here to hear it.

My pleasure builds as I feel his fingers at my entrance, and with one quick move, they fill me.

"Holy shit," I pant as my hands tangle in his hair, pulling him tighter against me.

He sucks hard on my clit as his fingers continue their steady rhythm, and I ride out my orgasm.

"Get some rest, baby," he says as he leans back on his hands, licking my juices off his lips. "Because that was just the beginning."

"So, how's it been living with Nancy?" I ask as Dominic wraps his arms around me.

Last night, Dominic woke me up, more than once, giving me the best orgasms of my life.

And who was I to complain?

I've woken up today feeling much better. Still sick, but better.

"It's been ... testing," he says, tensing.

"You're both still adjusting. I mean, how long has it been since someone has lived with you?"

"Years," he says flatly.

"Exactly, and it's probably the same with her, too." I force a laugh, hoping to lighten the situation.

It took me a while to get used to living with the girls. They were different from my parents and Jason. "Give it a couple of weeks, and hopefully she'll be back home."

He hums, and I feel his chest rumble beneath me. "I've never known someone to have as many deliveries as she does."

"What does she have delivered?" I ask.

"What doesn't she?" I can hear his frown without even looking at him. "She has four boxes a day. A fucking day."

Four boxes A DAY?!

"I opened one the other day, and it was some kind of light-up mask." His face scrunches up in confusion.

"Oh, you mean an infrared mask?"

He shrugs. "Who knows? I'm out of my element here."

"It's to keep us looking young," I say with a smile.

His hands tighten their hold around me. "I was thinking ... when you're better, we could go away. Our family owns a beautiful house in the Cotswolds."

"You want to go away? Together?" I can't help but tense.

"Yes, together," he says. "And I'd also like you to meet my parents this week."

I jump up, the blanket falling from me, leaving me bare. Dominic's eyes never stray from mine.

Brownie points.

"Are you fucking with me?" I ask, and his eyes immediately darken as his hands land on my bare thighs.

"Do you really want me to answer that question?"

I nod.

"No, I'm not fucking with you," he says firmly. "You're the first girlfriend I've ever had, and I'm still learning this shit as I go along. I don't know if I'm moving too fast, and quite frankly, I don't fucking care. I'm doing what I feel is right for us … and I want to spend some alone time with my girlfriend. And I want you to meet my parents."

My shoulders tense slightly.

"They know about you, they know what I feel towards you, and they want to meet you."

"They do?" I ask gently.

"Yes, Shortcake." He grips my hips and drags me above him, until I'm straddling him. I feel his cock beginning to harden beneath me, but I try not to focus on that and solely on his words.

But it's *hard.*

My hips wiggle slightly he brushes against me.

Dominic's hands tighten on my hips, his fingers digging into me. His cock brushes between my folds, and he lets out a hiss.

The sensation of him brushing between my slick folds, teasing me … it's too much.

He glides my hips forward and back against him.

"Is that a yes?" He pauses his movements, and I want to scream like a child.

"It's a yes." And with one quick thrust, he pushes himself inside me.

Chapter 31

Dominic

"How's Isabella?" Joey asks as we head to Giovanni's warehouse on the outskirts of London.

"She's good."

"Then what's gotten up your ass?" he says, and my head whips in his direction.

"Maybe being summoned to the lion's fucking den." I flex my hand on the door handle and sigh. "I don't know how to explain this part of my life to her."

"Oh …" He draws out the word. "Yeah, you're on your own there."

It's not something you can speak about over a morning cup of tea. She isn't like us; she's normal.

I scrub my hands down my face.

"What do we know?" I ask, changing the subject.

"All I know is that our brother fucked up, yet again," Joey says.

Being summoned to Giovanni's warehouse is never a good sign.

"He went to sort some shit, and he ended up killing ten men. Ten *trained* men."

Fuck.

Once we reach the huge metal gates, the security checks our IDs before giving the nod. The gates open with a screech, and our car glides through the lavish estate.

We pass numerous security details, each carrying military weapons, until we reach the warehouse. Louis, our driver, heads straight for the metal doors, stopping right in front of them.

"We will be back shortly," I say, and he nods as we climb out.

The warehouse is huge, but it's run down. A metal table sits to the left, old red leather chairs situated around it, as Giovanni stands at the head, waiting.

"Nice of you to join us," Giovanni says.

"Giovanni," I say, giving him a nod. A quick glance around confirms Alessandro isn't here.

"Do you know why I've summoned you?" he asks.

"Alessandro," I say, annoyed.

"Correct," he says, twisting his knife on the end of his finger. "I sent him in to do one job. One. Fucking. Job," he shouts, slamming his fists on the table. "And now we have a war on our hands."

I swallow.

"I'm sure if Nico and I go to see Garcia—" Joey begins, but Giovanni raises his hand, cutting him off.

"I can't let this go unpunished." Giovanni nods towards the black van in the corner. Three of his men stand in front of it. One swings the back door open, and they reach inside and drag a beat-up and gagged man out, flinging him onto the floor.

Alessandro.

He grunts at the impact of his body hitting the ground.

I dart forward, but strong hands wrap around my arms and tug me back. The cold barrel of a gun presses against my skull.

"Don't move, Nico. It won't end well for you," Giovanni says, smiling.

"Tell them to release me, Gio, or I promise you, I will kill them with my bare hands."

He nods his head, and his hands drop, but the gun remains.

"Nico, please behave, and the gun will disappear," Giovanni says calmly as he nods his head to his men, who lift my brother into a standing position, and he hisses. His face is covered in blood from a cut above his eye. "Your brother here needs to remember his position."

My eyes clash with Alessandro's.

"I have set a meeting up with Garcia. You will go there, and you will fix this. Have I made myself clear?"

"Mr. Barone," Garcia says as he takes a seat at his desk. "What a pleasure."

"Garcia," I say, clasping my hands in my lap. "I appreciate you seeing me today, considering the circumstances."

"Yes," he says with not a hint of empathy. "The poor families."

Garcia is a slippery little shit, and he doesn't give a fuck about anyone but himself.

"I'm here to smooth things over."

"How?" he asks as he leans back in his chair, the leather creaking under his weight.

He may be a powerful man, the head of his family, and feared by many, but there's one thing Garcia will never have.

Respect.

The people in this world don't respect a man who hits his wife, and it's common knowledge that Garcia has been doing it since the moment they signed on the dotted line.

"I would like to compensate you and the families for my brother's mistake."

"Mistake?" he asks, raising his eyebrow. "It seems to me your brother knew exactly what he was doing." His face reddens in anger as he rests his hands on his belly, the buttons straining.

"Like I said," I say sternly as I straighten my blazer. "I'm here to offer compensation. Giovanni is prepared to offer a significant cash payout. Think seven figures. Fuck it—make it eight."

He shakes his head, his cigar dangling from his fingers. "That's not enough, Nico. You see, it's got me thinking. What do I want?" He taps the cigar on the ashtray. "And what I want is Alessandro."

Silence fills the air.

"To what end?"

"It seems your brother's fate is in your hands, Nico. Execution, or joining the family on a more ... official basis."

My brow furrows. "Official?"

"What a beautiful thing, to merge our two families in holy matrimony. My daughter, Georgina, is in need of a husband. I can think of no better match."

Chapter 32

Dominic

Giovanni: Take Garcia's deal.

Me: It isn't your decision to make.

Giovanni: Alessandro is a liability. A liability I'm ready to be done with.

Giovanni: Or choose execution. What do I care?

"Hello, son." My mother presses a light kiss to my cheek as she enters Romano's. She chose the restaurant, already booking a table before I had a chance to ask Isabella.

"Mum," I say, smiling, before shaking my father's hand. He presses a kiss to my cheek before standing back. "Where's Alessandro?" I ask, checking over their shoulders once more.

"He said he'd meet us here," my father says, shaking his head.

Things are still a little tense between the two of us, since I've had to sort his mess yet again.

Tonight is about one thing, and one thing only: introducing Isabella into the family.

"Come on," I say as I glance over my shoulder at Isabella, who's fidgeting with her charm bracelet. "I want you to meet my girl."

My mother smiles widely as she walks ahead of me.

"Hello Isabella. It's lovely to meet you. I'm Katherine." My mother smiles widely as she engulfs Isabella in a hug. Her arms lay stiffly by her side for a few seconds before she hugs my mother back, her shoulders dropping as she finally relaxes.

"Hello Isabella. I'm Tomasso," my father says as Mum finally lets Isabella go and takes her seat.

Isabella shoots me a smile as I pull out her chair for her before taking the adjacent seat.

"So, Isabella," my mother says as she takes a sip of her wine. "Dominic mentioned you like to paint."

She nods. "I do. Do you paint?"

"Sometimes, when the mood takes me," my mother says sadly.

My mother used to paint all the time, people mainly, but she lost her muse after her sister suddenly passed away a few years ago.

"I'd love to see some of your work," Isabella says.

"I would love that, darling. Please, anytime." My mother smiles. "But enough about me ... tell me more about your work."

"I paint landscapes, mainly. I enjoy painting lakes, flowers, anything with different tones of colour."

I can't wait for her to see my grandparents' garden.

"Dominic—drink?" My father nods his head towards the bar, and I stand, pressing a kiss to Isabella's head.

"I'll be back in a minute, Shortcake." She smiles as she continues to speak to my mother.

My father nods to the barmaid, who begins pouring us a whiskey. "I heard about this business with Alessandro and Garcia ... what has Giovanni decided?"

My jaw clenches. "We're taking the deal."

My father's knuckles turn white as he gulps his drink. "Then he's made the right decision."

My brother takes that moment to stride into the restaurant, beelining straight for the table.

"Come on, your brother is here," my father says, tapping me on the shoulder and darting over. "Alessandro, nice of you to join us."

The bruises on his face are more prominent now. The cut above his eye is healing well.

"I told you; I'm a busy man," he bites out, his eyes drifting over Isabella.

Isabella's eyes widen at my brother's attitude.

He intimidates most people.

It's the darkness that surrounds him. That "don't give a fuck" attitude for everything in life. But I don't want that for Isabella. I want her to feel comfortable around my family.

I pull her chair closer to mine and drape my arm over the back of it.

"Shortcake, this grumpy piece of shit is my younger brother, Alessandro."

She smiles at my words.

"Hi," she says to him, and he lifts his chin in recognition.

"Don't worry about him," I whisper in her ear. "He can be an arsehole."

She smiles but doesn't reply. "Are you ok?" she asks. "What did your father want?"

"Not now," I say, clasping her hand in mine and squeezing it.

She tenses.

The waitresses start bringing the food my mother preordered, covering the table in various dishes.

"So, Isabella. How did you meet my son?" my mother asks, gaining her attention.

"We met at a nightclub," Isabella says nervously. I squeeze her hand in reassurance under the table. "But since then, he seems to be everywhere."

My mother chuckles. "He does like to insert himself into your life. Grace told me everything about you, and I knew the moment I met you that I would adore you."

Isabella's cheeks redden.

"I'm glad you approve, Mother."

"More than approve." She smiles widely, sending me a look.

She's already planning the wedding.

"So, what do you do for work?

Isabella's hand freezes for a moment as she reaches for the pasta. "I'm a waitress," she mutters quietly.

"Oh, I bet that's fun," my mother says, and Isabella's eyes snap to hers in surprise. "Back when I was younger, before I met Tomasso"—she pats my father's hand—"I was a waitress. It was some of the best years of my life."

I smile as I watch her hang on to my parents' every word as they tell her how they met.

I have never done anything like this before. I didn't even have second dates, so this is new for me.

But all the while I feel my brother's eyes on me.

Chapter 33

Isabella

Ollie: How are you? You're not answering my calls.

Ollie: Call me back. Where are you?

Ollie: Phoebe told me you're away.

Ollie: You're with that Dom guy, aren't you?

"We're here," Dominic says beside me as the car comes to a halt outside a beautiful white building. A huge glass terrace runs the whole width of the house.

Tall oak trees sit off to the side, revealing a peek of the lake beyond. My mouth drops open, and I rip open the car door. The smell of fresh-cut grass hits me immediately.

My feet tug me towards the terrace.

This place is beautiful.

A stone-built wood burner sits to the side, with wicker chairs looking out over the lake.

"I told you it was beautiful," Dominic says behind me.

It really is.

"Come inside when you're ready. I would love to show you the rest," he says, before I hear the stones crunching under his feet as he heads back to the car to grab our bags.

Since the meal with his parents last night, things have been a little tense.

Dominic is hiding something from me.

He left the table with his father for a while, and when they returned, things weren't the same. He was distant, distracted. So, I've been doing what I always do: protecting myself. Withdrawing just like he is.

A soft bark sounds behind me as Buddy explores the huge grounds, disappearing into the bushes.

A huge wooden fence wraps around the grounds, blocking anyone from seeing inside.

"Come on, Buddy," I say over my shoulder as I walk carefully over the stones. "Let's go help your daddy bring the bags in."

Buddy catches up to me just as Dominic places the bags by the front door.

His eyes light up at my approach. “You're going to love it here,” he says as he pushes the door open and ushers me to enter first.

My eyes immediately land on the oak beams and the matching staircase that sit right in the middle of the grand foyer. Old wooden flooring runs throughout.

“It has eight bedrooms, four bathrooms, and two sitting rooms,” Dominic says behind me.

I nod. “That’s good. We can have a room each.”

Dominic freezes behind me.

I know I’m being a bitch. But I can’t seem to help it.

“I know things have been tense since meeting my parents,” he says, taking a small step towards me. “I promise you I will tell you everything. Tonight. At dinner.”

I reluctantly nod.

“I would love to see our room ... if that’s ok?”

We head further into the house, climbing the stairs. The huge glass panels let in so much light, and my steps falter as I admire the view from the second floor.

“You should see it when it snows,” Dominic mumbles.

He leaves me standing there as he heads down the corridor. I quickly catch up to him as he opens a door. My mouth drops open as I enter the room.

A four-poster bed sits to my right, white crisp sheets with pink piping. A huge white soft rug sits in the middle of two sofas and a stone log burner. I walk towards the terrace, opening the doors and looking out at the picturesque views below.

Greenery for miles.

All I see is the tops of the trees and nothing else.

Pure silence.

It's perfect.

"Each room has its own bathroom ... with a bath," he says with a hint of a smile. He knows I'm a sucker for a bathtub. "I'll leave you to ... settle in," he says as he takes a step towards the door before he looks over his shoulder at me. "I will cook us dinner tonight – I think we should talk then."

I nod as he closes the door.

And only then do I let out the breath I was holding as I throw myself on top of the bed.

"Look, give him a chance to explain," Sam says down the phone as I lie on the bed staring up at the ceiling.

"I don't know what to do."

"If you don't, I think you'll regret it for the rest of your life," Chloe says. "Has he lied to you so far?"

I shake my head, even though they can't see me.

"Exactly. The guy has been an open book." Chloe sighs. "Yes, he changed during dinner, but from what you said, his brother was an asshole."

She's right there. Alessandro is a grade-one asshole.

"Get yourself all dressed up, then go downstairs like the boss bitch you are with your head up and your tits up and hear him out."

I push into a seated position, looking at myself in the mirror.

"Put on the matching underwear I hid in your bag, too," Sam interjects, and my brows pinch.

"What matching underwear?"

"It's hidden in the zipper at the front."

I tune Sam out as I push off the bed, grab my bag, and open the zip. I pull out a bright red lace set.

"Wow."

"It's beautiful, isn't it?" Sam mumbles down the phone as I lay the underwear out on the bed. "I saw it in the shop the other day and I knew you were going away, so you're welcome."

A chuckle slips free as I perch on the bed, my hand drifting over the lace.

"Now, go show Dominic what he's missing."

"I second that," Chloe adds

"Love you," we all say in unison as I cut the call and quickly get ready.

The smell of chicken tikka masala makes my mouth water the moment my foot hits the bottom step. I've spent the last hour locked up in my room speaking to my girls. I was avoiding the tense conversation I knew was about to happen.

Things could go one way or another.

I could either hear him out and everything goes back to the way it was, or I'll be calling an Uber.

"Wow," Dominic says the moment I enter the living room. His eyes drift slowly over me, and my skin heats instantly.

Traitor.

Giving his head a subtle shake, he slides a strawberry daiquiri towards me on the kitchen island.

"Wow, it smells amazing." I do a little happy dance inside at my choice of outfit—a cute red dress with matching slippers.

"Thanks," he responds as he starts plating up the food before reaching into the oven and taking out a huge naan. "Please, take a seat outside. There are blankets."

I follow his eyeline, and my breath hitches.

Candles flicker in the wind as Dominic rounds the island, his hand resting on the small of my back as he steers me outside.

The huge wooden table is covered with candles and four huge bouquets of bright red roses. Dom pulls out a chair, and I take a seat, and he drapes a fluffy blanket over my legs, his face inches from mine as he stares into my eyes. "Are you warm enough?" he whispers, and I nod.

I tear my eyes away from his and break the spell.

My heart screams at me.

But my head thanks me.

"I'll go get the food," he says in a clipped tone before he disappears inside.

Soft music plays from the speakers as I look out at the lake. The light glistens against the water from the moon.

The leaves rustle in the breeze as the wind begins to pick up, leaving a soft chill in the air. I pull the blanket around myself.

"Here you go, Shortcake," Dominic says, drawing my attention to him as he places the plates on the table before taking a seat next to me.

"Thank you."

We tuck into the food in silence, the only noise the music and my heart beating wildly against my chest. Once we finish, Dominic takes the plates inside and places a plate of freshly baked cookies on the table.

He clasps his hands together. His black, long-sleeve T-shirt strains against his arms as he stares into my eyes. "When I was growing up, my father and uncle sold drugs on a dangerous family's territory." His shoulders tense as I sit in silence. "Our family has been forced to work for the mafia since ... which in turn means Alessandro and I do." He pauses, his words sinking in.

The mafia?

"It's not something I had planned in my life, but it is what it is. I've learnt to live with it. I don't get my hands dirty; I just use my skills from my work in law."

I open my mouth to speak, but no words come out.

What is there to say?

"There is no out in this life, Isabella." He leans across the table and reaches for my hand. "But I just want you to know that you will always be safe with me."

He squeezes my hand lightly, his eyes pleading with me to say something.

But what can you say when your boyfriend informs you that they work alongside the fucking mafia?

I take a deep breath.

"I don't want any secrets between us. None," I whisper, staring down at my hands.

"None," Dominic confirms as he reaches for my hand and places it on his thigh, interlocking our fingers.

"Now, can we just enjoy my first ever holiday?"

Chapter 34

Isabella

Ollie: When are you home?

Ollie: Will you be coming to art class?

"You must be crazy," I shake my head in disbelief.

"Come on." He tugs me by the hand towards the hot tub.

I shake my head again.

There is no way I'm getting in; it's freezing outside.

Dom stops right in front of the hot tub as his hand drops from mine. "Then I guess I'll have to go in—alone." He tugs his shirt over his head and drops it on the wicker chair. My eyes threaten to drift to his broad shoulders, but I manage to stop myself.

I didn't realise how much I needed this break. How much *we* needed it.

I've learnt so much more about him and his family over the past week, and it's reassuring that there are no more secrets between us.

Dropping down on the wicker chair, I tug the blanket around me as I watch Dominic shed his clothes. He leaves just his boxers on before he climbs into the hot tub. His eyes never waver from mine.

"Get in, Isabella," he orders, making a shiver run down my spine.

"I think I'm ok here, thanks," I breathe, dropping the blanket from my shoulder.

His eyes darken.

"What are you wearing, Shortcake?" he asks, his eyes following my every move as I drop the blanket more, revealing a bright red bikini top. "Isabella," he warns as his hands tighten around the top of the hot tub.

I rise to my feet and drop the blanket completely.

Dominic lets out a harsh breath.

"I mean it, Isabella ... get in here, or I'm getting out."

I shake my head again.

He rises to his feet, and I shriek, darting forward. "Ok, ok, I'm getting in."

He holds out his hand as I step in and tugs me towards him.

"I think I've fallen in love with you, Isabella Bennett."

My breath hitches.

The water warms me instantly as his hands cup my face. "You don't need to say it back."

"I love you too."

His brows jump in surprise.

I close the distance between us, my lips brushing his, and the moment they do, he lifts me into his arms and deepens the kiss. I gasp into his mouth as his hands glide down my body and grip my ass.

He rocks his hips against me, and my eyes flutter closed at the friction. "Dom, please."

"Say it again," he says as his hand dips under my bikini bottoms, brushing against my sex.

My breath catches in my throat.

"Say. It."

"Say what?" I groan as he teases my entrance before pushing his fingers inside of me.

"You know what, baby." His teeth graze my jaw.

"I love you."

His fingers massage my walls as I continue to grind my hips down on him, the pleasure building

"Fuck, baby. The best sound in the world," he growls, his fingers curling inside of me as I pant, "is the sound of you whimpering in my ear."

His words tip me over the edge as my mouth parts, my skin on fire.

I'm pretty sure I'm addicted. Addicted to my boyfriend, whom I've just told I love.

He pulls his fingers from me and tugs down my bikini bottoms before I feel him pushing at my entrance.

His eyes flare the moment I wrap around him. "Fuck," he hisses.

Curling his hand around the back of my neck, he presses his lips against mine.

My skin prickles as he continues to drive into me—hard. The water splashes over the sides as a layer of sweat forms across my forehead.

I dig my nails into his shoulders, and I moan into his mouth.

A wave of electricity rushes through me as I drive my hips down against him.

Waves of water lap around us, and I can feel the pleasure rippling through me, my walls squeezing him as he inhales sharply. He stills, his hands gripping me tightly as he finds his own release.

"Fuck, baby." He chuckles softly, his breath fanning against my lips as he rests his forehead against mine. "Who knew hot-tub sex would be so hot?"

A laugh rips through me.

He pulls himself free of me before passing me a strawberry daiquiri.

"Penny for your thoughts?" he asks, drawing my attention to him.

"I was just thinking about how different we are."

He scoots closer to me. "Tell me what's on your mind, Shortcake."

"It's just ... look at you ..." I say quietly. "Look at this place. Your family. And I'm just permanently living in my overdraft." I let out a chuckle, but it has no humour behind it.

"Shortcake," he says, taking my glass from me and placing it onto the side before clasping my hands. "I don't want you to worry about that ... it makes no difference to me."

That's what a wealthy person says.

"I don't want to be a trophy wife or a baby machine. I have my own goals."

A laugh slips past his lips. "And I support those goals. I want you to become a successful artist so I can play golf all day." He winks.

My lips curve into a smile as I relax.

He tugs me closer as I lean back against his chest.

"I mean it, Shortcake. I want you for you."

I sigh.

"I'm sad we're heading home tomorrow."

"We can stay a little longer, if you'd like?"

I shake my head. "No, I need to get back. Phoebe has already been kind enough to let me have these days off. I can't push it."

"Well, this place isn't going anywhere," he says with a smile. "We can come back whenever you'd like."

My eyes drift over the garden. "I'd really love that."

Chapter 35

Dominic

Joey: Are you home today or tomorrow?

Joey: If you keep ignoring me, I will call you until you answer.

Joey: Never mind, I checked on the tracker and noticed you're on your way home. See you tomorrow, buttercup.

Joey: Don't forget the coffee and my present.

"Hello?" I answer quietly on speakerphone, Isabella sleeping in the passenger seat next to me.

"Dominic, it's Charles." I'm instantly alert.

"Is everything ok?" I say calmly as I weave through the traffic.

"I don't know how to say this, but ..." He pauses for a few seconds as I hear him clear his throat. "It's Nancy. She hasn't been home in three days. Hasn't been at your office, either. I've tried to call her, but her phone goes straight to voicemail."

"What?" I say, my hands tense on the steering wheel.

"Sir ... I know you're away on holiday, but I think you need to be here. The police are on the way."

"I won't be long," I rush out as I hit the gas.

The moment we pull up, Isabella stirs, rubbing her eyes.

"Baby," I say, and she jolts fully awake. "I need you to stay in the car and lock the door."

"What's going on, Dom?" she rushes out, panicked, and I want to wrap my arms around her, but Nancy needs me right now. "You're scaring me."

"It's Nancy ... something's happened."

Unclasping my seatbelt, I climb out. "Lock the door, and no matter what, don't leave this car."

She nods, and I pause just long enough outside to hear her lock the door before I take off running.

I head straight for the security office and push the door open. Charles jumps to his feet the moment he spots me, Kingston standing behind him.

"Barone," he says, giving me a nod. "We've found something on the CCTV. The most recent sighting of her. Take a seat."

I do, and he hits play.

It's early morning footage, eerily quiet, from the street outside the building.

After a few seconds, Nancy comes into view, striding in those ridiculously high heels she wears. She turns her face back, a look of fear on it, before disappearing out of frame.

A moment later, another figure appears, face covered in a balaclava.

Kingston pauses the footage.

"Fuck," I say, scrubbing my hands down my face.

I shouldn't have left her alone.

Chapter 36

Dominic

Nancy has been missing for three days.

Her father would be turning in his grave.

"I'm just going to get into the bath," Isabella says as she takes off her apron after baking another batch of cookies.

She seems to have started a new hobby—stress baking. Unfortunately, baking isn't a skill she possesses. The last batch nearly broke my front tooth.

"Ok, baby. I've got a call to make and then I'll join you," I say, pressing a kiss to the top of her head as I watch her disappear down the corridor.

"Barone," Giovanni says on the second ring. "What do I owe this pleasure?"

I'm almost certain this is a call I'll regret, but if anyone has the power and influence to find anyone in this city, it's Giovanni.

"Nancy is missing." My hand tightens around my phone.

"And you're telling me this because ...?"

The guy is an arrogant bastard.

"Because in case you've forgotten, Nancy is now a part of your payroll," I bark out.

I pinch the bridge of my nose at the lack of empathy this guy has for anyone in his life.

"I'll see what I can do," he says, bored, cutting the call. It makes me want to throw my phone across the room, but instead, I drop it to the counter and head into the bathroom. My eyes land immediately on Isabella, her back to me, as she stares out at the lights of Knightsbridge while relaxing in the bathtub, the bubbles cover her completely.

I shed my clothing. "Sit forward, Shortcake."

Her breath catches as she jolts forward, her eyes wide. "You scared me."

I climb in behind her, pulling her against my chest as she leans back against me and we look out at the city together.

"Who were you on the phone with?"

"Giovanni. I ... asked him to pull some strings," I say, stroking my hand down her arm, leaving goosebumps in my wake.

Isabella tries to turn around, but I stop her.

She sighs. “Will he find her?”

Fuck, I hope so. “Yes.”

She lets out a relieved breath as she tugs my arms tighter around her. She sinks deeper into the water, and the bubbles stick to her hair.

I play with her loose curls.

“Dom,” she whispers. “I know with everything going on, life can pass us by in a bit of a blur ... but you still need to look after yourself, too.”

“You have no idea how much you mean to me, Shortcake.”

Her breath hitches, her hand pausing its movements through the bubbles.

“Since the moment I met you, I knew you were different. Different from anyone I have ever met.” I wrap a curl around my finger. “I know we’re going through a lot right now, and I know I’m distracted, but I need you to know that no matter what, I will always look after you.”

She nods against me.

Dropping her curls, I stroke my hands up her stomach and cup her breasts. Her breath hitches, her nipple begging for my attention. I give it a light pinch, and she arches her back, pushing it further into my palm.

“Dom,” she moans, and it's music to my ears.

I glide my other hand down her beautiful body, dipping further into the water before I find my own piece of heaven, my fingers stroking between her thighs as she parts them for me. her head falling back on my chest as I push them inside her.

"This isn't going to be slow, baby ... as much as I want to take my time. I fucking can't," I say through clenched teeth.

She nods against me.

"Turn around," I whisper in her ear. I pull my hand free from between her thighs, and she obeys, straddling me. The water laps over the edge as she settles on top of me, her hands resting on my shoulders as she stares intensely into my eyes. Her beautiful, wet body brushes against mine as his lips brush my jaw. "Take what you need, Dom."

She gasps as I line myself up with her entrance, and with one quick thrust, I fill her.

Her hands tangle tightly in my hair as I lift her up and down on me, doing exactly as she asks.

A moan rips through her as she throws her head back, and I continue to drive her onto me.

I latch my mouth around her neck, her pulse beating rapidly beneath my touch as our bodies slap together.

We need this.

A strangled cry slips past her lips as her nails dig into my shoulders, cutting into me as she finds her release, gushing around me. I squeeze my eyes closed at the sensation and pick up the pace, my cock swelling inside as I continue to drive home.

My eyes land on her beautiful face, a glow touches her cheeks as her pussy clenches around me once more. A shiver runs down my spine as my cock jerks inside of her, and I find my release.

"Fuck." Isabella chuckles softly as she collapses onto my chest.

Mine.

Grabbing the back of her neck, I pull her up to me and whisper against her lips, "Marry me."

"What?" she rears back, her eyes widening.

"You heard me."

"Are you being serious?" She sits back, my cock already starting to harden again inside her.

If I could be buried inside her permanently, I would.

"As serious as a heart attack," I say, levelling my eyes with hers.

I want nothing more than to call her mine.

By any means possible.

Her eyes search mine as my words linger in the air.

"Shortcake—" I begin, but she cuts me off with a shake of the head.

"Yes," she mutters so quietly that I barely hear her.

"Did you just say yes?"

"I did." She gives me a watery smile, and I dart forward, cupping her face in my hands and closing the distance between us.

Chapter 37

Isabella

"So, how was the trip?" Georgina asks as we are two bottles of wine down.

"It was good," I say, blush colouring my cheeks. "I feel we really needed it. I feel so much closer to him now."

"I bet you *were* a lot closer to him," Sam jokes.

Dirty bitch.

Even if she is bang on the money.

"I hope you were closer to him, whilst also being *careful*," Phoebe says, nudging my foot under the table.

Tonight we've gathered at Wilson's in our pyjamas for girls' night, which involves gossiping but mostly planning the pop-up.

"Yes, you dirty bitches. I'm on the pill," I say, shaking my head.

Georgina fills my glass. "So, Gee, tell me ... are you in a secret relationship that we don't know about?"

"God, no." She snorts. "I have my career to focus on; I don't want to be saddled with a man right now."

"I think I need a goal in mind," Sam muses. "It feels like you all have your lives planned, and I'm just over here, hoping that one day I'll find a man who loves me, for me."

"You have plenty going for you." I brush off her worries. "Your party planning side hustle is just starting to take off. I can't wait to see what you do with this."

Her eyes light up instantly as she sits forward in her seat. "You'd better get that notepad out, Phoebe."

Phoebe dramatically opens her notepad, writing in extra-large letters, "Isabella's gallery."

"So, when are we doing this?" Sam looks at me, and I shrug. "A week from now? Two?"

That is the million-dollar question; I don't know.

Nancy is still missing, and no matter what excitement I feel about finally hosting my own exhibition, I can't let myself feel completely happy until I know she's ok. Nancy and I weren't close, and I'm not here pretending that we were, but no matter what, she will always be a huge part of Dominic's and his family's life. Which means I need to make the jealousy I feel towards her disappear. No matter what, it means she is in my life now.

“Let’s give it two weeks,” I say, a wave of guilt washing over me.

Last night, in the bathtub, was the first time since we got back that I’ve felt happy. And I woke up this morning to him kneeling by the bed, holding out a ring—a gold band with a gorgeous oval diamond.

“Anyway, guys,” I say, inhaling a deep breath for courage as everyone stares at me. “I have some news.”

“Oh God, what is it?” Sam says first.

“I’m engaged,” I say, holding out my hand towards them. The light hits the ring perfectly, making it glisten.

“Oh, my fucking God!” Chloe yells as she grabs my hand first, tears forming in her eyes. “You’re getting married!”

“I guess I am.” Now, it’s my turn for tears to form.

“Congratulations,” they all say in unison as they all jump up and hug me.

“Seems we have a wedding to plan now, too!” Phoebe says with a wink.

She loves a good party.

I chuckle softly. “Chloe and Sam … would you do the honour of agreeing to be my bridesmaids?”

I wait for their reaction, and after a few seconds, shrieks echo around the restaurant as they launch themselves at me.

I laugh. “I take that as a yes?”

“Yes,” they both cry into my hair.

"Shall I make all you lovely ladies a cup of tea? You know, to sober you up?" Manny asks, shaking his head at us all. I think it's safe to say we have all drunk a little too much tonight.

"Don't be a killjoy," Phoebe says, waving him off.

"I think that's a good idea," I say, jumping up and following him into the kitchen.

I hop up on the counter and watch as he takes out the cups. "At least you're sensible, Bel. I'll have to carry her home later."

I chuckle.

He isn't wrong.

"You look happy, kid," he says, smiling sweetly at me.

"That's because I am," I reply as I swing my legs. "I have a question to ask you, and I don't want you to feel pressured into anything, ok?"

He turns to face me, leaning against the counter. "Spit it out."

"Could you ... I mean, will you ... I would appreciate it if you would walk me down the aisle?"

His Adam's apple bobs, and for the first time since I've known him, tears well in his eyes. He pulls me into a fatherly hug. "I would be honoured."

"Thank you," I say, hugging him back, a lump forming in my throat.

Leaning back, he cups my face. "You know we see you as a daughter."

I smile tearfully. "You're the parents I always wanted."

"Isabe—"

Someone knocks on the back door, cutting Manny off. He frowns, shuffling over to pull it open. "What do you want?" he says gruffly, and I instantly feel sorry for whoever it is.

"I saw the light on, and thought Isabella might be here ..."

My smile drops.

Ollie.

"We're closed; you'll have to come back in the morning," Manny says sternly.

I appear behind him, placing my hand on his shoulder, and Ollie's eyes light up.

"Manny, it's fine." I squeeze between him and the door.

Manny gives me one final look before he pulls the door shut and leaves us alone.

"Thanks, Bella, for a second there I thought he was going to lock me out here," Ollie says, and I turn to face him. His usual clean-shaven face has a few days' worth of stubble, and he looks exhausted.

"Ollie, are you ok?"

"Of course I am," he says, batting off my worry as he paces in front of me, his hands firmly tucked into his jeans pockets.

"You look—" My words die in my mouth as he pauses, and his eyes drop down to my pyjamas. He frowns.

"Is there a reason you're wearing pyjamas?"

"Yeah." I let out a nervous chuckle, pulling my cardigan tighter around me. "It's girls' night."

"Right." He sighs, as he rocks on his feet. "I've been calling and messaging you."

"I'm sorry.

"Why did you ignore me?"

"I didn't, I was just busy."

He doesn't seem his normal self.

He seems jumpy; his eyes keep flicking behind me.

"Ollie, what's wrong?" I take a step closer.

"What's wrong?" He scoffs. My brows pinch together. "Where have you been?"

"I went away for a few days," I say, swallowing.

"With that Dominic, no doubt."

"Well ... yes. He and I are together." I play with the charms on my bracelet.

He reaches out and twists a curl between his fingers. I want to pull away, but I can't. "I thought you were different, Bella. But you're just a typical Stacey, wanting to be kept by a rich, older guy."

I blink, no words forming.

What the hell is he talking about?

"You need to come with me." He jolts out, wrapping his fingers around my arm and squeezing tightly. "I need to get you away from these Chads."

"Ollie, please, you're hurting me," I say quietly. I try tugging my arm free, but he just squeezes it tighter, and I try not to wince.

He ignores me. "You'll never be his."

"Ollie. I'll ask you nicely. Let. Me. Go," I say sternly this time. Worry is clawing its way up my throat, but I bat it down. I don't want Ollie to think he has any upper hand on me.

"I've waited long enough for you," he says. His eyes are wild.

I shake my head. "Ollie, please. You're scaring me."

He closes the distance between us, and I stand frozen in my spot.

"You will be coming with me," he says, his hand wrapping tightly around my arm as he squeezes it to the point of pain.

I wince. "Let me go."

"I will never let you go," he says through gritted teeth as he tugs my clothes, and I lose my footing slightly and stumble.

I rip my arm free and take a step back, but he advances on me, his hand rearing back before he slaps it hard across my face. Copper fills my mouth.

"You made me do that, Isabella," he says as he takes another step closer. "Love makes you do crazy things ..."

He reaches for me again, but this time, there's a loud clanging noise before he slumps forward, falling to the ground.

"Get the fuck off my daughter," Manny booms, holding his frying pan in the air. He tugs me behind him. "Are you ok?"

I nod.

His brows pinch together as he reaches up, his thumb grazing my bottom lip, and I wince again. There's blood on his finger.

"I'm going to call the police," he says as I step back, pulling his phone out of his pocket.

Ollie tries to get up, but Manny holds the frying pan higher, and he freezes.

"Yes, police, please," Manny says as I tune him out, wrapping my arms around myself.

Within minutes, a truck screeches to an abrupt halt, and the door swings open.

My mouth drops open as Kingston moves at speed, grabbing Ollie around the neck and tackling him to the floor before shoving cuffs roughly around his wrists.

He lowers his voice, his usual calm demeanour gone, replaced with an anger I wouldn't have thought possible. "You lay another hand on Isabella again, and I will kill you."

A siren sounds behind us, and two officers dart out of a second car, grabbing Ollie off Kingston before shoving him in the back.

Kingston straightens his blazer. "I'll be there in a moment," he says to his colleagues, who nod, before he turns to face me, his eyes darkening as they zone in on my lip. "I've called Nico. He's on his way ... but in the meantime, I need to know exactly what happened."

"Manny and I were in the kitchen when there was a knock at the door. It was Ollie, so I came out, and he spouted some stuff about me and him and Dominic." I shrug. "I'm not sure he's in his right mind. He called me Stacey." Kingston freezes, his eyes narrowing, but I continue. "Then he ... he ..."

"It's ok, Bel," Manny reassures me as he wraps his arm around my shoulder, giving me a small smile.

"He hit me." I let out a breath, tears stinging my eyes. "I haven't told anyone, but Ollie has been sending me messages for a few weeks. Some are fine, but others are ..." I pull my phone out of my bag, unlock it and pull up the message thread, and hand it over to Kingston.

His brows pinch. "Fuck," he mutters before his eyes clash with mine. "Why didn't you report this?"

"There was nothing to report." I shrug. "I thought I could handle it."

"You should have told me," Manny says, hurt on his face.

"I'm sorry. I didn't want to worry anyone," I rush out. "Please, just get him the help he needs."

Kingston frowns before nodding. "I need to get him to the station. I'll call you tomorrow for a full statement," he says, his hand hovering over my arm for a moment before he pulls it away.

Chapter 38

Dominic

"I take it you're not here as my lawyer?" Ollie says sarcastically, cuffed to the table in the middle of the room—the only thing stopping me from killing him with my bare hands.

The legs of the chair scrape on the cold stone floor as I take a seat opposite him, undoing the buttons on my blazer.

Silence fills the air; the only noise is from the clinking of his cuffs every time his hands move.

"Look, Dominic, we both know why you're here," he says, and I arch my eyebrow, waiting for him to enlighten me.

Because in this very moment, I want a round of fucking applause that I haven't rammed that paper cup down his throat and choked him.

"It's because your girlfriend has feelings for me."

"My fiancée," I correct him, and I watch his face redden in anger.

He snaps his mouth shut. His Adam's apple bobs up and down before he speaks again.

"Fiancée?" He spits out the word, and I nod, a wave of satisfaction running through me as his hands tense in his cuffs.

"Since when?" he bites out.

"Since I fucked a yes out of her."

I smirk as the colour drains from Ollie's face.

"Now, I'm here to inform you that I am going to make it my life's mission to get you the longest sentence I possibly can. I'm also going to make sure to put you in the same prison as Isabella's brother. You think I'm bad?" My laugh echoes off the walls. "Just you wait."

Chapter 39

Dominic

"Be careful, King. If you carry on, you'll wear a hole in your floor," I say as I take a seat at his desk.

Kingston pauses his pacing and lets out a frustrated breath.

I thought seeing Ollie would calm the war inside of me, but it's only made it worse.

"Did you get what you wanted out of that fucker?" he asks, the vein in his neck pulsating as he takes a seat on his desk.

"No. I wanted to watch the life drain out of his body," I say, shrugging. "But obviously you had officers watching me from the glass."

I loosen my tie as I reach for his coffee and take a sip, the liquid burning my throat on the way down.

"Nico, do you know what the incel movement is?"

I shake my head.

He tugs at his collar. "The 'involuntarily celibate.' They're a bunch of losers who sit behind their computers all day. They like to blame women for the fact that they can't get a date."

I sit silently, letting his words sink in.

"They're mostly harmless, but sometimes there have been some cases where things can get ... violent."

I shake my head. "I don't understand what this has to do with anything."

"Ollie called Isabella 'Stacey.'"

"Stacey?" I ask, confused.

"Yes, Nico." He sighs. "In incel terms, a 'Stacey' is your typical attractive woman."

"Fuck," I say, slamming my hands down on his desk. "You're telling me that Ollie is part of this ... cult?"

His mouth opens, but my phone rings, cutting him off. I check it to make sure it's not Isabella calling, but Giovanni's name flashes on the screen.

"Now's not a good time," I say by way of greeting.

"Barone," he says calmly. "You'll want to hear this."

I pinch the bridge of my nose. "I'm listening."

"We've been looking into your little problem, as you requested. Does the name Oliver Preston ring any bells to you?"

About twenty minutes later, we're pulling up outside Ollie's estate—the building looks like it should be torn down and rebuilt, the bricks chipped and paint faded.

Children play outside, kicking a ball around without a care in the world.

We make our way up to Ollie's flat—third on the left, with dirty yellow curtains in the window.

There's an old, dirty sofa situated right outside his front door. Flat 4D.

Before we can try the door, an elderly lady pokes her head out of the flat next door. "Can I help you?" she asks, her voice croaky, like she's spent years chain-smoking.

"I'm here to see a friend." I say the words, and they instantly leave a foul taste in my mouth.

She narrows her eyes. "Who's your friend?"

"Oliver Preston."

At the mention of his name, her face scrunches up. "Tell him if all that banging carries on, I'll call the police on his ass. I don't care if I was friends with his bloody mother. God rest her soul."

I arch my eyebrow, nodding at her. "I'll pass that on. Thanks."

As soon as her head disappears back inside, Kingston kicks the door open, and it crumbles beneath his feet.

I follow him inside.

There's a worn mattress pressed against the wall—no covers, just a single pillow and a thin blanket. A plastic garden chair faces the single-glazed window, with a view over the car park.

Making my way over to the tiny wooden desk sitting by the one single door, which I presume is the bathroom, my eyes land on photos that are scattered over the desk.

Isabella.

Every single fucking picture is of Isabella.

Isabella at work.

Isabella at the supermarket.

Isabella at art class.

"Fuck." Kingston mutters behind me as my hand flicks through the pictures he has of Isabella. He pulls an evidence bag out of his pocket and slips the photos inside.

A small bang makes my head whip in the direction of the door in the corner. Kingston frowns.

There's silence, until we hear it again.

I try the handle, but it's locked. My brows pinch.

Who locks their bathroom door?

Kingston nods tightly at me before he kicks the door in with his foot.

It's pitch black. There's no window, no air.

I reach around the wall until my hand reaches the light, and once it's on, all my breath leaves me.

Nancy.

I rush towards her, pulling the rope out of her mouth, and her eyes snap open.

"Nance?" I say quietly as I bend at the knees, brushing her dark, greasy hair off her face. "I'm here, Nancy," I say softly. Her eyes are wild as they land on mine, and I see the relief flood her features before she starts sobbing, frantically trying to pull the handcuffs off, but they're fixed to the radiator.

It takes us seconds to get her uncuffed before she throws herself at me, and I catch her.

As soon as the ambulance pulls up to the hospital, Nancy's wheeled away into a private room, away from us while they check her injuries.

"Fuck." I tug at my hair as I drop down into a seat in the waiting room.

Guilt hits me. I always knew there was something off with Ollie, but I put it down to the jealousy I felt towards his and Isabella's friendship.

"Nico, we weren't supposed to know she was there," Kingston says as he sits next to me. "But we have her now, and she's ok." There's a slight shake to his hand as he grips his phone.

A few minutes later, a small voice speaks, making me whip my head up. "Dominic?" A nurse stands in front of me as I rise to my feet. "Nancy is asking for you."

When I'm led to Nancy's room, she looks much more like herself—except the spark in her eyes is gone.

"Nico." She gives me a watery smile. "I want to say thank you for coming for me."

"What have the doctors said?" I manage to say past the lump in my throat.

"Nothing much," she says, her hands gripping the blanket tight. "Just that I'll have a sore head for a few days. Severe dehydration. And it will take a while for all my bruises to disappear." She lifts her wrists, and I see bruises covering them from the cuffs. "Have you found Ollie?"

I nod my head. "He's in custody."

"He kept me locked up in the dark." A single tear slips down her cheek as I take a seat in the armchair next to her. A sob wracks through her. "What did I do to him?" She wipes under her eyes, and I zone in on the marks around her wrists.

"You did nothing," I say, reassuring her. "He's fucked in the head."

She nods.

"I need to know what happened, Nancy," I add as her eyes clash with mine. "Kingston is going to be in here soon, and he will want a statement."

Her eyes flicker outside. Dark clouds have started to form, rain hitting her window.

"He didn't *touch* me, if that's what you're asking," she says, and the relief hits me immediately. "I had an important meeting to get ready for ... and I knew the office would be quiet, so I decided to head there. How stupid am I? I walked down the street alone, first thing in the morning, when there was no one around." Her head drops into her hands.

"I just remember waking up in his place, cuffed in the bathroom," she says, scratching her forehead. "He would just scream at me, that you stole something from him, and that he needed to steal something from you."

My hands begin to shake in my lap as I shake them out. "You're safe now," I reassure her as I lean across, reaching for her hand, but she flinches, tucking her hands under the blanket.

"You're the reason I hung on," she says, her voice full of emotion, tears dripping down her face. "I need to know something ..."

"Anything?" I lean forward, and she sinks further into the bed, shrinking away from me.

"Nico, I love you."

My body tenses as I let her words sink in.

Her brows pinch as her hands tangle in the blanket.

"You don't love me back, do you?" she mumbles.

I shake my head.

"Do you think you ever could?

"I don't. I'm sorry."

"God," she says, scrubbing her hands down her face. "I've been so fucking stupid. I've pictured us ending up together since we were children. Yes, you fuck other women, and yes, Isabella came onto the scene, but I just thought you may have been having some fun."

"I'm sorry, Nancy."

She holds up her hand, cutting me off. "There is no need to be sorry. You can't help how you feel." Her chin drops down to her chest. "I think it's best you leave."

My eyes snap to hers.

"I don't think you should be left alone."

"I'm not alone," she rushes out. "I have the doctors and nurses," she adds before staring at the wall in front of her.

I stand, straightening my sleeves. "I'll be back first thing in the morning." I turn on my heel, heading for the door.

"Don't." Her words stop me in my tracks. "I want a clean break, Nico. I think I need it. So, please, don't come back here. I think I'm going to take some time for myself. Go away for a bit."

"You don't need to do that." I take a step closer, but she shakes her head, smiling softly.

"Goodbye, Nico."

I get an Uber back to my car, and the moment I've sank back down on my familiar leather seat, I slam my hand against the steering wheel.

After what he's done ... as long as he's out there, Bella will never be safe. She'll always be looking over her shoulder.

I hesitate a beat before picking up my phone and hitting dial.

"Hello, brother," Alessandro says on the second ring. "To what do I owe this pleasure?"

"I need you to make someone disappear."

There's a pause.

"Consider it done."

Chapter 40

Isabella

"Shortcake, where are you?" Dominic says the moment the door to his penthouse clicks shut. His footsteps echo off the tiles as he heads further into the kitchen.

I peek my head from beneath the blanket on the sofa, where I'm cuddled up with Buddy. "I'm here," I say quietly, and his eyes find mine.

Taking out his keys and phone from his pocket, he places them onto the glass sideboard before closing the distance between us in a few quick strides. He sits down in front of me on the coffee table. "Are you ok? I'm sorry, I took longer than expected."

"It's fine. I was grateful for the quiet," I say with a shrug. "And this little guy has been keeping me company."

As much as I would have preferred to have him here with me, I know there were things he had to sort out.

In other words, Kingston got him five minutes alone with Ollie.

I'm not stupid.

I hear a sharp inhale of breath as his hand snaps out, gripping my chin and tugging me close. “He fucking touched you?”

I sigh. “Dom, please. It's fine.”

“It's not fucking fine,” he growls, his eyes going to a dark shade of blue.

“Dom,” I say loudly as he drops my chin and begins to stand, but my hand snaps out, stopping him. His eyes meet mine. “Please, I’m just glad you’re here.”

His eyes soften as his thumb strokes my lip gently. “Fuck, baby, I’m sorry. I should have come straight home—”

“You have nothing to be sorry for,” I say, wrapping my hand around his wrist, and tears begin to sting the backs of my eyes. “You had things to sort. I understand. Anyway, Kingston said he’s going to get Ollie the help he needs.”

Something passes over Dominic’s face before it disappears just as quickly as it came.

“Shortcake, I need to tell you something.”

Dread runs through me at the tone of his voice.

I try to pull my hand free, but he doesn’t allow it.

“We’ve found Nancy.”

“What?!” I say, my eyebrows shooting into my hairline. “Where is she? Is she ok?”

“Shortcake ...” He lets out a heavy sigh. “It was Ollie. All of it was Ollie.”

His words take a moment to sink in.

No. I shake my head. He doesn't even know her. It doesn't make any sense.

"Baby, he was the one stalking her."

Why would he stalk her?

It doesn't make any sense.

Dom begins to shake in anger. "I went to his flat. He had pictures of you ..."

"What kind of pictures?" I say my breath is coming out low.

"All sorts, baby. He's been watching you since the moment he met you."

I sit up straight, the blanket falling from me as Dominic sits back.

He reaches for my hand, grounding me.

"He's fucked in the head, Shortcake. I ..."

"You what?"

A shadow crosses over his face. He tugs me close so I'm perched on the end of the sofa.

"You don't need to worry about him anymore," he whispers into my hair.

"What do you mean?" My brows pull together.

He pulls back, shooting me a look. "You know what I mean, baby."

Dominic's eyes search mine, and without warning, I throw myself into his arms. All the emotions from the day rush to the surface as my tears fall freely.

I'm not just crying for me.

I'm crying for the friend I thought I had in Ollie.

I'm crying for Nancy ... for what he put her through.

I cry for it all, as Dominic hugs me tight and reminds me of why I love him.

He is my home.

Chapter 41

Isabella - Two weeks later

“Oh, Bel. We're so proud of you,” Phoebe says, squeezing my arm.

It's finally here—my little pop-up.

And my heart is full.

They closed Wilson's for the afternoon, and we spent the time getting everything ready for tonight, pushing all the tables to the back to leave the space open. Sam purchased crisp white sheets and hung them on every wall, before placing all my pieces of art in front of them on wooden stands. Each has its own price—something I had no input on because Dominic insisted on going through that himself with Sam.

“If we can do this with such short notice, imagine what we could do if you gave us full rein to plan the wedding?" Sam says with a wink before Manny ushers her from the other side of the room.

She's like a dog with a bone.

"Isabella!" Katherine and Tomasso give me a quick hug. "This is amazing!" Katherine says, her eyes dancing around at my work.

"Thanks," I say, blushing.

"I hope you've brought your chequebook," Katherine jokes, slapping Tomasso on the chest. "I'm going to be buying it all." She chuckles softly, steering her husband away, admiring the painting I did of their Cotswolds house.

"Are you ok?" Chloe asks as she links her arm through mine, steering me through the people, who nod as we pass.

"Yeah, it's just a lot," I say, clearing the lump threatening to form in my throat.

"You've been through a lot," she says, squeezing my hand.

She isn't wrong.

"There you are," Dominic says, smiling as he tugs me towards him and tucks me under his chin. "Baby, you look beautiful." His eyes drift over the soft gold satin dress. The material hugs my body; a small slit runs up the side, revealing my leg with every step.

"Thank you," I say, heat rushing to my cheeks at the intensity in his eyes. It's the look he gives me when he wants to get me naked—and if it weren't *my* night tonight, I'd let him.

"It's a good turnout," he says tightly as he fixes his tie.

It's more people than I ever expected.

"I know; it's making me nervous." I let out an awkward chuckle.

Dom's hands wrap around my waist, and he tugs me flush against him. "I'm so fucking proud of you, Shortcake." He closes the distance between us as he presses a light kiss to my lips. My arms wrap around his neck as I melt into him.

"Enough of that," Chloe says, and I step back, blush hitting my cheeks.

"Jill is taking pictures, so make sure you put on your best smile," Phoebe says out the side of her mouth as she passes, flicking her head to the side.

Her friend Jill's camera goes off repeatedly as she glides around the room.

Dominic holds me tight, his eyes flicking around the crowd of people.

The soft hum of chatter fills the room as people admire my work.

My work—God, I never thought I would hear the day I said that.

Pride rushes through me.

"Come on, Shortcake. There's someone I would like to introduce you to," he whispers as he guides me through the people. An older, vibrantly dressed lady comes into view as she stares intently at a painting of a mountain range. "Amelia," he says, and at the mention of her name, she turns around. Her eyes lit up.

"Dominic," she says softly, her green eyes flicking to me. "And you must be Isabella. I've heard so much about you."

"Hi," I say quietly as I place my hand in hers. "I'm sorry; you have me at a disadvantage ..."

Surprise touches her face. "Well, I apologise for that. I'm Amelia. I own an art gallery in Soho."

My mouth threatens to drop open.

"A good friend told me there was a new, up-and-coming artist, and I wanted to get in here first."

Up-and-coming ... am I dreaming?

"I see how you work, and I like it." Her eyes drift over the painting next to us of the open sea. The different shades of blue lap together as the waves hit the light sandy shore, the sun glistening over the waves. "Tell me, where did you train?"

My mouth opens and closes a few times, my nerves clawing their way up my throat. Dominic wraps his arm around my waist, squeezing it. He gives me a warm smile.

"I'm mostly self-taught, but I've been going to a class for the last few weeks."

She nods.

"How many times a week?"

"Once."

She hums, her bright orange nail tapping on her lips. "That needs to be increased. I like you, Isabella," she says, her eyes drifting behind me, before landing back on mine. "I will be in touch. Dominic—always a pleasure to see you."

My brows pinch together.

She gives me one final look before leaving.

"Did she owe you a favour or something?" I ask, shrugging out of his hold. "Is she one of your *mafia* friends?"

A crease appears on his forehead as he tucks his hands into his trouser pockets. "A favour?"

"Yes," I hiss. "Because it seems suspicious that you dragged a literal gallery owner here, and then she tells me she likes my work. I need a drink," I say as I spin on my heel and weave my way through everyone, leaving him standing there, staring after me.

The night ends better than I expect.

I sold six pieces, and my emotions are working overtime as I tried to hold back the tears.

"Lock up, will you, sweetie?" Phoebe says as she passes. "Manny and I are wiped out."

"Of course," I reply as Manny places Phoebe's coat on her shoulders. My eyes automatically land on Dominic, who leans against the bar, nursing a whiskey.

"Bye, guys!" they shout over their shoulders as the door clicks shut.

I click the lock into place and finally let out a breath.

Gathering some empty wine glasses, I place them onto the counter.

"Are you ready to talk to me yet?" Dominic says.

My shoulders drop as I turn to face him. "What is there to say?"

His mouth snaps shut.

"I really thought she liked me ... liked my work." I scoff. "But really, she only came tonight for you."

He pushes off the counter and storms towards me.

His knuckle brushes beneath my chin, tilting my head up as he looks into my eyes. "Baby, she fell in love with your work because it's fucking amazing. You're fucking amazing."

"Dom—"

"No, listen to me," he says, his eyes flicking between mine as his breath fans across my lips.

"Amelia is a hard nut to crack, and you did that. Not me. You. Sometimes you do this, you doubt yourself, and it drives me fucking wild ... because you don't see what I see. What everyone sees."

"What's that?" I ask breathlessly, my heart beating fast.

"The most beautiful, talented artist I have ever known."

A laugh rips through me.

"I mean it, baby, I can see a bright future for you, and I'm going to be there holding your hand every single step of the way."

His hand wraps around the back of my neck as he closes the distance between us, crushing me against his chest.

All the anger I felt moments ago disappears as I match the intensity of the kiss.

My hands tug his hair tightly, and he growls into my mouth.

He sweeps everything on the table to the floor and pushes me against it, his body covering mine as his hands stroke down the silky material of my dress.

Our breaths mix as his eyes darken.

"Tell me you love me," he growls against my neck.

My heart pounds in my chest as he bites down.

"Tell me."

"I love you, Dominic," I say breathlessly.

A smile covers his face. "You're mine, Isabella, and I'm so fucking proud of you," he whispers against my pulse.

I moan, throwing my head back as he roughly gathers my dress, pulling it over my head and dropping it to the floor.

His eyes darken as he sees my white lace underwear.

"Fuck, Shortcake ... if I knew you were wearing these, I wouldn't have lasted the night," he groans, his fingertips stroking me over them.

His touch ignites flames inside of me, my whole body on fire.

"Dom, please!"

"I love it when you beg." He brushes his hand against my panties, and his pupils dilate.

Silence fills the air as he pauses, staring down at my body.

"What's wrong?"

"I just want to look at you," he says, studying every inch of me. "You're so perfect."

My breath hitches.

His hands stroke up my body, grasping mine and pinning them over my head as he peppers kisses across my chest, teasing my nipples through my bra as I arch my back off the table.

"Dom, please don't tease me," I plead, and I feel him smile before he reaches behind me and unclasps my bra.

The moment it's off, his mouth latches around my nipple, and I groan.

He releases my hands, skimming his fingers down my sides before I feel them brush between my thighs.

I squeeze my eyes closed as he parts my folds and he rubs circles over my clit. "Oh God," I moan.

"Open your eyes, baby," he says, and I do. "I want you to watch me as I make you come."

A smirk tugs at his lips as he pushes himself down my body, before he sends me a wink and buries his head between my thighs, sucking my clit into his mouth as his fingers plunge further inside of me.

My hands fly down, tangling in his hair, and I hold him tight against me.

He doesn't hold back as he feasts like a starved man, and I lap it up, loving every single second, his eyes never wavering from mine

A wave of electricity shoots through me as my thighs squeeze his head, but he doesn't stop until I've ridden out my orgasm.

"Baby, there is no better taste in this world than you on my tongue," he says, licking my juices off his lips. He pulls himself free of his trousers. Precum glistens on his tip as he works himself, his eyes on my pussy. "Look how wet you are, baby," he growls. "You're dripping."

He pushes his tip inside of me before pulling back out, repeating the motion.

"Dom!" I scream in frustration; a chuckle rips through him before he pushes completely inside of me.

My eyes roll into the back of my head as I wrap my legs around his waist.

"I've been thinking," he growls as he picks up his pace. "I want you to move in with me."

"You do?" I ask as he continues to pound into me, the pleasure is building inside me as the table scrapes across the floor with every thrust.

"Say yes," he grunts, his shoulders tensing.

"Only if you're sure?"

"Never been so sure of anything in my life," he rasps against my lips. The moment his tongue strokes mine and I taste myself, pleasure rips through me.

"Fuck." He groans as he spills himself inside of me.

The only noise is our heavy breathing as he buries his face in my neck, peppering me with kisses before he pulls himself free.

"I mean it, Isabella," he says as he fixes his trousers, and I fix my skirt. "I want you to move in with me. Tonight."

Chapter 42

Dominic

"Why don't you tell me why you're here, Nico? We are both busy men, and it's unlike you to turn up without a meeting scheduled." Giovanni says as he leans back in his chair.

He's right, I don't normally turn up without an appointment, but needs must. And as much as I didn't want to owe Giovanni a favour, I have no other choice.

"Jason Bennett."

"Ah, yes," he says. "I hear congratulations are in order. Pity I had to hear about your engagement from your brother."

I grit my teeth.

"Let me guess. You want early release for your fiancée's brother, a man serving time for armed robbery."

"Your guess is correct," I say tightly.

Picking up his coffee, he takes a sip. "Mr. Bennett will struggle with ... employment, upon his release."

I open my mouth to speak, but he cuts me off, a sinister smile on his face.

"I'll secure his release. But I'll also secure his employment."

I shake my head. "Not happening, De Luca."

"It's not up for discussion," he says quietly as he twists his knife on his thumb. The blade glistens as the sunlight hits it.

I shake my head.

Isabella will never forgive me if I put her brother in harm's way.

"I'll be down an enforcer the moment your brother marries the Garcia girl."

"It's not up for discussion, De Luca." I try to protest, but he raises his hand. "Your brother is set to marry in twelve months. That gives Bennett a chance to learn his place. Get up to speed."

I flex my hand on my lap. "He's in prison, Giovanni," I say through gritted teeth. "I don't want him ending up back where he came from."

"Then you'd better make sure you keep him in check. And perhaps do a better job of it than you have with Alessandro."

Chapter 43

Isabella

"Hello?" a small female voice says on the other end of the phone as I pour myself my morning cup of tea. "Is that Isabella?"

Buddy brushes against my legs as he whimpers for his food.

"It is," I say, frowning. "I'm sorry, who is this?"

"It's Amelia. Amelia White. We met the other night."

"Yes!" I say a little too loudly, and she chuckles.

Way to play it cool, Isabella.

"Sorry, I didn't mean to scream down the phone. How can I help?"

"I was just giving you a call to say that I haven't been able to stop thinking about your art."

I pause. Am I dreaming? I pinch my cheek.

Nope, I'm wide awake.

"If you're free—"

"I am!" I blurt out before she has a chance to finish.

She chuckles harder this time. "Isabella, you are a character. I like you."

Character. That's one word for me.

"If you're free today, I'd love to meet you for lunch or a coffee?"

"I'd love to," I say, my hands shaking as my heart beats rapidly. Am I having a heart attack?

"Ok, I'll send you the address and I'll see you at twelve," she confirms before cutting the call.

I let out the scream I was holding.

Shit! I need to get Chloe here stat to make me look presentable.

Grabbing my phone, I dial her number.

"Hello?" she answers, muffled.

"Have you just woken up?" I ask.

"Damn right." She lets out a yawn. "What's up?"

"I need you to come over and make me look pretty."

I bite down on my nail as I wait for her reply.

"When?"

"Now."

Silence fills the air for a few seconds. "Give me half an hour."

God, I love her.

Exactly thirty minutes later, Chloe turns up a bag full of makeup in one hand and clothes in the other.

"I couldn't come empty-handed," she says, holding them both up before I shut the door behind her, and she gets straight to it, ushering me into the chair in front of her.

The moment my ass touches it, she begins work, tugging at my hair.

"Ouch!"

"Stop moaning, baby." She scoffs as she plugs in the straighteners. "You were the one who woke me up, so I'm getting my own back."

"Bitch," I mumble to myself as she sections my hair into pieces and straightens it to the best of her ability. Once she's finished, she begins my makeup. "So, who are you meeting?" She yawns for the fifth time.

"Amelia ... Amelia White." I try to hide my excitement, but it brims over.

"Babe, I don't know who that is," she replies as she starts on my eyeshadow, adding light brown tones to bring out the blue in my eyes. This girl is a magician.

"She's just this amazing woman ... who owns her own art gallery."

The moment the words leave my mouth, Chloe's hand freezes and she rears back.

"Her *own* art gallery?"

"Yes. Her *own*." My lips curve into a smile.

"Why didn't you say that?" she blurts out. "We need you to look as professional as possible. Have you got your portfolio ready?"

"Yes. It's already by the front door."

"Please don't forget it," she says, shooting me a look.

"Isabella!" Amelia smiles widely as I make my way over to her table, shaking her hand.

It isn't your usual place; each wall is decorated in beautiful flowers, fairy lights weaving perfectly between them. The carpet is green, designed to give the illusion that you're walking on grass.

"I'm sorry, I wasn't sure what you would like, so I ordered us a glass of wine each. Is that your portfolio?" she asks before taking a sip of her wine, her eyes dropping down to the pink folder in front of me.

I nod.

She holds out her hand towards me. "Can I have a look, please?"

I sit in silence as she opens it, her eyes scanning over every piece.

"You're very talented, Bella," she says, not looking up from my work. "Very talented."

"Thank you," I say as I feel my cheeks beginning to redden.

She returns my smile as her hands drift over my line work. "I called you today because," she says, her eyes flicking to mine, "I would like to offer you an apprenticeship at my gallery."

My mouth drops open. "An apprenticeship?"

She nods. "I think it would be beneficial for you to come and work alongside me."

I nod, a lump forming in my throat.

"Everyone has to start somewhere. I am very impressed with your work, and I think with the right teacher, you could really go somewhere."

A smile tugs at my lips. "That would be ... amazing."

"Excellent!" she exclaims, causing a few people to look our way. "We are going to get on like a house on fire, my girl."

Chapter 44

Isabella

"Isabella, is that you?"

My breath hitches at the sound of my mother's voice. A voice I haven't heard in years—not since I ran.

A voice I had almost forgotten.

My feet are rooted to the spot.

"Hi, Mum," I manage to breathe out. I hold the kitchen side for support.

"It is you." She lets out a sigh of relief.

Why is she calling me after all this time?

She clears her throat, the tension between us thick. "I think you need to come home."

I inhale slowly. There's no reason for me to ever go back there.

"I just can't believe you didn't come back for the funeral."

"The funeral?" I manage.

"Your *father*'s funeral. Some daughter you turned out to be."

My breath leaves me in a whoosh at her words.

"I didn't know, Mum."

And with that, she cuts the call.

"Is everything ok?" Dominic asks, having caught the tail end of the conversation. Pouring himself a coffee, he leans against the kitchen counter, Buddy trying to nibble the hem of his trousers. He's like Dom's little shadow.

"Yeah," I say, my brows pulling together as I stare down at the blank screen on my phone. "That was my mother."

"Your mother?" he asks as he lets out a cough. "What did she want?"

"My dad died."

"What?" His eyes widen as he closes the distance between us, pulling me into his arms. "I'm sorry, Shortcake."

Buddy scratches at our legs as I bend down and lift him into my arms.

It's true what they say, pets really can feel our emotions.

"It's fine." I hug him back, resting my head against his chest as I breathe him in.

"Are you going to go back?"

"I don't know." I pull back, and he cups my face.

"Whatever you want to do, I'll support you. Whatever you decide."

"What would you do?"

His hands drop from my face as I hop up on the kitchen counter, and he stands in front of me, his hands resting on my thighs.

"I think ... I would go. See if I could get some closure."

My shoulders drop.

Closure? Is there such a thing when it comes to my parents?

"She could have changed." His hands rub my thighs reassuringly. "Or maybe she is the same, but you will never know until you go there."

I shrug, my eyes flicking to the TV with the local news playing.

"At least go say goodbye to your dad."

"I missed the funeral," I choke out.

He pulls me against him, his arms a solid, grounding presence.

"I ... I think I want to go back."

Chapter 45

Isabella

"Are you sure you don't want me to come in with you?" Dominic asks, as he presses a kiss to my knuckles.

"I'm sure," I say confidently, even though I feel anything but. "I need to do this alone."

"I'll be here if you need me," he says as I tug my hand free and open the car door.

I stand at the end of the driveway, my eyes flicking towards the overgrowing weeds.

"Hello, Isabella," my mother says as she stands stiffly by the front door, dragging her eyes over me.

"Hello, Mum." Her once bright blonde hair, now lifeless, a bright grey and unruly, pinned to the top of her head by an elastic band. Her light blue eyes don't hold the same sparkle they used to, as she continues to stare at me.

"You look ..." My mother's eyes flick down my body. "Different, yet the same."

I let out a nervous chuckle. "Yeah."

She turns around and heads inside, leaving me standing on the edge of the driveway.

I take a deep breath, all my nerves rushing to the surface, as my palms begin to sweat. I rub them on my jeans as I head inside, shutting the door behind me.

Nothing has changed.

The old, mismatched sofas still sit in the middle of the room. The wooden coffee table still has all the burnt rings on it, and the small TV still sits in the corner on the TV stand, a layer of dust covering it. On the windowsill is the only picture there is of the four of us. The only picture where we are all smiling. I remember the day it was taken as if it were yesterday.

I pick up the picture, admiring it, my finger tracing Jason's face.

"Would you like a drink?" Mum yells from the kitchen, drawing my attention to her.

I place the picture back in its spot and head in to find her.

"I'll have a cup of tea if that's ok?" I say, my voice sounding small as I take a seat at the table.

She nods, pulling out mugs from the cabinet above.

I wind my hands tight in my lap as I twist the ring on my finger.

"So, how have you been? What has it been, seven years?"

"I've been fine, thank you," I say, brushing off her final question. It doesn't matter how long it's been.

They say bricks and mortar don't make a home; a person does. And there has never been a truer sentence.

"That's good. You look good. You've gained weight."

That's what good food does to you. I want to say, but keep my mouth closed.

Her eyes brush over me before she places my tea on the table and takes a seat.

"How did it happen?" I ask, a lump forming in my throat.

I've never been close to my parents, and that's something I've come to live with ... but it's still a shock that he's really gone.

"He had a heart attack."

I nod. "When?"

"Eight weeks ago."

Eight weeks, yet she only called me yesterday.

I nod again, my hands wrapping around my mug. The heat burns my hands, but I need it to ground me.

"Can I ask where you've been the past few years?"

"London," I say, my eyes focusing on the ring stains on the top of the cup.

She nods. “Are you happy?”

“I’m getting married next month, actually.”

Her eyes widen in surprise. “Next month?”

I nod, choosing not to give her any more information.

People dream about their wedding days from such a young age. Having their mum help them plan it, be a part of every single detail ... and yet, my mother doesn’t even ask my fiancé's name.

“Is your brother ... is he ok?” she asks softly, changing the subject.

I nod.

She lets out a frustrated breath at my lack of cooperation.

I owe this woman nothing.

The only family I need is back in London.

Chapter 46

Isabella - One month later

"You look beautiful," Sam says behind me as she clasps the necklace around my neck.

The diamond sits perfectly on my chest.

"It's beautiful," Chloe says, smiling.

Dominic had it sent to our hotel room this morning—a thin gold chain with a beautiful oval-shaped diamond, the same as my engagement ring.

"I love it," I say, my emotions threatening to spill over since the moment I opened my eyes this morning.

Standing in front of the full-length mirror, I admire the beauty of the wedding dress I've chosen—a beautiful A-line, satin dress.

Today is supposed to be the happiest day of my life, and the only thing I can think about is Jason.

"He would want you to be happy," Sam says softly as she squeezes my hand, her eyes meeting mine in the mirror.

"I know," I say, my voice cracking.

Chloe presses a quick kiss to my cheek. “Right, girl, we will meet you out there.” She turns to Sam, clasping her hand. “Let's give her a minute,” she whispers.

Sam looks at me one last time before she follows Chloe out. I wait until the door clicks shut before I let out the breath I was holding.

I press my fingers against the necklace again, a smile tugging at my lips.

Dominic is more than thoughtful, constantly thinking of me even when I don’t think of myself.

Someone knocks softly on the door, not waiting for me to call them in.

“Squirt?”

My breath hitches, my hands flying to my mouth.

Jason?

“Wow,” my brother breathes, his eyes taking me in as he stands behind me.

A navy suit clings to his body, a pink handkerchief matching the bridesmaid dresses.

“How... how are you here?” My words come out weakly. I turn, my heel catches on my dress, and I stumble. Jason catches me effortlessly, my hands landing on his chest.

He tucks a piece of my hair behind my ear, my eyes meeting his, and I see the tears in his eyes. “You look ... you look beautiful, Squirt.”

My heart beats against my chest, my tears flowing freely. “How?”

“That fiancé of yours.” He grins, his fingers wiping the tears away. “He’s been coming to see me weekly, making a case ... fuck Bel. He’s good. He got all charges dropped.” He smiles softly.

“I can't believe you’re here.” I try to get my emotions in check as I take a deep breath. “Enough, Isabella,” I mutter to myself. “Maura will kill you if you wreck her handiwork.”

“Who’s Maura?” Jase asks, his brows pinching together.

“She’s the lady who did this.” I gesture down to my dress, my makeup, my hair. “Anyway, enough of that ...” My eyes flick to the clock on the wall, and I gasp as I gather my dress and lift it, rushing towards the door. “I have ten minutes to make it down the aisle before Dom comes looking for me, and you know he will.”

“Oh, I know.” Jason chuckles softly. “The guy seriously loves you.”

I grin over my shoulder. “Does this mean you finally approve?”

He strides towards me, grabbing the train of my dress. “Let's not push it.”

“We are gathered here today …” the priest begins, but I tune him out as I stare at my soon-to-be husband.

He looks so handsome in his signature navy suit and crisp white shirt, the final touch his pink handkerchief in his pocket. Buddy is sitting directly by his feet, in a matching suit, his tail wagging as he stares up at me.

“Isabella … Shortcake,” he says, his eyes flickering down my body before landing back on mine. “I vow to always be there for you, through everything. To always support you in everything you do. To love you unconditionally.”

Tears drip down my face onto my dress as I try to control my breathing. No one likes to see a blubbering bride on their wedding day.

“You’ve come into my life like a steamroller, throwing it into complete chaos.”

He chuckles softly before continuing. “But I wouldn’t have it any other way. You have made me realise that there is a life outside of the office, and I can’t wait to explore it all with you by my side.”

Everyone around the room is crying as they stare at us.

He reaches inside his blazer, passing me a tissue, as I dab it under my eyes.

"So, I say I do, Isabella, today, tomorrow, and every day for the rest of our lives."

I smile widely as he slides the gold diamond-encrusted band onto my finger before pressing a kiss to it. "Now, Isabella ..."

I take a deep breath, retrieving Dom's ring from Sam. "Dominic, I want to thank you ... Thank you for not giving up on me. I know things haven't been plain sailing ... but it has made me realise that no matter what life throws at us, with you by my side I can take it on."

Dominic smiles, tears glistening in his eyes as his hand squeezes mine.

"You have shown me what true, unconditional love is, and for that, I will always be loyal to you. Protect you, and beyond anything else, love you." I tear my eyes away from his as I slide a simple gold band onto his finger. "You say that I am yours, but in turn that also makes you mine, so, I do, Dominic Barone."

"With that, I pronounce you man and wife. You may kiss the bride."

Epilogue

Dominic

"Everyone, raise your glasses to Mr. and Mrs Barone!"

Everyone does so, but I can't bring myself to smile.

I have a feeling I know exactly what's about to be unleashed.

My eyes drift over everyone as they pay attention to my father, the respected man, but what they don't know are the secrets that hide beneath.

Isabella squeezes my hand, drawing my attention to her. She gives me a warm smile, and I stare at the person who means the most to me. My wife.

"Today is extra special for our family," my father says, cutting his eyes to me before his mask slips firmly in place. "Not only are we celebrating one union, but two. Our youngest son, Alessandro, will be marrying the beautiful Georgina Garcia."

My eyes snap to Alessandro, who leans against the bar, gripping his glass tightly in his hand.

I look around the room, listening to the excited murmurs at the thought of another celebration. Giovanni catches my eye as he sits in the corner, grinning widely, raising his glass to me.

He always has loved the chaos.

"So, if we can raise our glasses for a second time, to Alessandro and Georgina," my father says as he finishes the contents of his drink.

I remain still as Georgina pushes up and storms out of the room.

"I'll be right back," Isabella mumbles.

I watch them disappear as all the guests rush out into the garden.

"What the fuck are you playing at, old man?" I hear my brother's voice as he stands in our father's face. I rush to them, pushing at Alessandro's chest.

"Not here," I say quietly to him.

His eyes cut to mine. "Were you in on this?"

I sigh. "It was for your own protection."

"Fuck you," he barks out, hurt flickering across his face for a millisecond before his mask slides firmly back into place.

He spins on his heel and storms out.

Fuck. I pinch the bridge of my nose as I take a deep breath.

"I apologise, but my hands were tied," my father says behind me, flicking his head towards Giovanni. I don't bother turning around.

"I told you, not fucking today," I say, my jaw ticking as I stare at my father. A shadow passes across his face, and his lips remain in a thin line. "I need to go fix this," I add before turning on my heel and chasing after Alessandro.

Georgina stands with her hands on her hips next to my wife in the bathroom as she glares at my brother. "Fuck you, Alessandro."

"In your dreams," he bites back, and Georgina's face morphs into disgust.

"Never in your fucking life ... you, you, piece of shit," she shrieks, slipping off her heel and throwing it at him, but he catches it effortlessly.

"That's no way to talk to your fiancé."

"I think you two need to speak in private," I say, gaining their attention. "Go to my office. You'll have some privacy there."

Georgina lets out a huff before pushing past me, Alessandro hot on her heels.

Once we're alone, I close the distance between Isabella and me.

"What the fuck is happening?" Isabella asks, looking at me for the answers, but today isn't the day. "Georgina is ... mafia?"

I cup her face in my hands as I lower my voice. "I don't want anything to wreck today for us. I promise to tell you everything ... but please, don't ask me today. Today is about us."

Her eyes search my face, and just when I think she's going to protest and push me for information, she does the complete opposite and nods.

I press my lips against hers, and she instantly melts into me.

This kiss is raw, possessive, and passionate, all mixed into one. I take out all my frustration on her lips, and she lets me, matching me.

Gripping her ass, I lift her and place her onto the counter as I stand between her legs.

"Tell me, Mrs Barone," I whisper against her delicate neck. "Do you want me to make you scream now, later, or both?"

"Both."

"My greedy, greedy wife." I smile against her neck as her breath hitches. My hands glide beneath her beautiful wedding dress, reaching her lace panties. I groan, pulling them down her legs and dropping them at my feet.

My fingers brush against her wet pussy, and her eyes flutter closed.

"I love you, wife," I say as I push a finger inside of her, before adding another, easing them in and out.

"Dom," she cries, her pleasure building. The redness on her cheeks appears, like it does every time she's close.

She rocks her hips against my hand, the roughness of my palm rubbing against her clit.

"Come on my fingers, baby," I growl into her ear, goosebumps dance along her skin. "That's it."

Her head falls onto my chest as her orgasm rips through her, her pussy squeezing my fingers tight.

I pull them from her wet heat, bringing them to my lips to suck off her juices.

She watches me with hooded eyes, biting her lip before quickly reaching forward and fumbling with my trousers.

It's only a few seconds before my thick, hard cock springs free, her hand squeezing me tight.

Lining me up with her entrance, she sinks onto me, inch by inch, until I'm completely inside her.

"Wait, baby," I say as I reach into my pocket and pull out a little friend. A micro bullet.

Her eyes widen as she stares at it, licking her lips. "Is that what I think it is?"

I nod as I switch it on, and it vibrates in my fingers.

Her eyes flare with desire as I reach between us, pressing it against her sensitive clit. The moment it comes into contact, a cry slips past her lips, and she throws her head back.

She gasps. "You've had this in your pocket all day?"

I nod. "Burning a hole, waiting to be used on my wife."

She smiles, a look of pure pleasure on her face.

I give her a few seconds before I begin moving, holding the bullet firmly against her as I pick up my pace. She's slick with arousal as I pull myself nearly out, before ramming back inside. Her hands grip my arms painfully tight as she hisses, her skin glowing with sweat as I continue my assault.

She comes with a scream, and I'm not far behind her.

The only sound is our heavy breathing and the low hum of the music down the hall.

BANG!

My head snaps up.

"What the hell was that?" Isabella asks, breathless, as I pull out of her and tuck myself into my trousers.

"Shortcake, stay in here and lock the door," I rush out as I stroke her cheek reassuringly.

"Was that a gunshot?"

"Yes."

Her hand flies to her mouth.

"Stay here. Lock the door," I say as I grip her chin. She doesn't answer me as she stares blankly at the door. "Shortcake, are you listening?"

She nods.

I pull open the door and wait on the other side until I hear the lock click into place before darting towards the noise. Screams are coming from downstairs, but I head off towards my office.

I rip open the door, my steps coming to a sudden halt as I spot Georgina holding a gun, her chest rising and falling in quick waves.

"Georgina?" I say, trying to gain her attention.

"You fucking shot me!" my brother says, and my head whips in that direction.

Alessandro sits on the floor, blood dripping from his arm.

"It's just a graze," Georgina sings, the gun falling to the floor at her feet. "Stop being such a baby."

"Al, are you ok?"

"Do I look ok?" he bites out, his glare focused on Georgina.

"Listen—" she begins, but she's cut off as the door to my office bursts open and people pile in.

"Call the doctor!" my father yells as he drops to his knees at Alessandro's side.

"He doesn't need a doctor." Georgina scoffs, and my father whips around to face her. She takes a step closer to him, her eyes focused on Alessandro. "I promise you,

Tomasso. If you go ahead with this marriage, I will kill him."

She spins on her heel and storms from the room, slamming the door behind her.

Acknowledgements

I would like to thank many people for their support during this journey.

Thank you to my friends and family for understanding that I need to retreat whenever possible to perfect this story, and for understanding that it takes time. I apologise for saying *I'm tired* for the millionth time.

Thank you to my mom, Susan, for giving me the nudge I needed, and listening to me daily speaking about my idea's and never getting bored. I thank you. <3

I want to thank my amazing editor, Evelyn, at Pinpoint Edit, for not just being my editor, but my friend. Putting up with my crazy ass and helping me every step of the way. From talking through ideas late at night, to calming me down when I'm having a panic. I couldn't have done it without you! <3

I want to thank the incredible Giulia at Ever After PR for being truly fantastic. You have also become a friend to me and have helped me immensely. From my graphics to my Arcs, but mainly with my cover –

I couldn't have achieved it without you. You've been wonderful, taking ideas and bringing them to life in the way you have. <3

I want to thank my amazing proof-reader, Alex, at Eros Edits. She is not just a friend but a fellow indie author, too. She has been amazing during my journey and has helped me whenever I needed it. <3

I want to thank my amazing boys, Kyle and Rowen. They have been brilliant, letting me speak about my characters like they are real people, and for understanding that I need to write, edit, and also have a meltdown about my book every so often. <3

And last but not least. Thank you to my biggest supporter, my love, my best friend, and my husband, Scott. You have been the most amazing, supportive, and the most helpful person I could have ever asked for. Listening to me speak about all my crazy ideas I have, thank you for keeping me on track whenever I want to throw in the towel. I couldn't love my family more for giving me the strength I needed. <3

I also want to take the time to thank the friends I have made along the way ... helping me, supporting me and answering any questions I might have. I couldn't have done it without you all. <3

Finally, I want to thank you, my readers.

The reason I write is to give you an escape from reality and to fall in love with the stories that live rent-free inside my head. I really hope you enjoy every story. <3

Readers

I hope you enjoyed reading Dominic and Isabella's story as much as I did writing it.

If you would like to find out more about Alessandro & Georgina then there story will be released 2026.

Forever His:

https://www.amazon.co.uk/dp/B0FWZZC34Z

If you fell in love with Nancy her story will be coming December 2025:

Forever Unexpected:

https://www.amazon.co.uk/dp/B0FX16NTRW

For more information on any upcoming books or simply to tag me in any of your posts ... Then please feel free to follow me on Instagram.

https://emmalstevensauthor.com/emma-l-stevens

@EMMALSTEVENS_AUTHOR

Printed in Dunstable, United Kingdom

74545290R00190